TALES FROM

Hymn-ă-dry-ăs

FIGHTING TO SURVIVE

JONATHAN HAMBRIDGE

ISBN 978-1-956010-29-9 (paperback)
ISBN 978-1-956010-30-5 (hardcover)
ISBN 978-1-956010-31-2 (digital)

Copyright © 2021 by Jonathan Hambridge

All rights reserved. No part of this publication may be reproduced, distributed, or transmitted in any form or by any means, including photocopying, recording, or other electronic or mechanical methods without the prior written permission of the publisher. For permission requests, solicit the publisher via the address below.

Rushmore Press LLC
1 800 460 9188
www.rushmorepress.com

Printed in the United States of America

IN THIS THE Second Generation of the First Age, a Great Evil prevailed and overtook the land. I, Āi-ās, Heir of Stră-thōn, Son of the Ă-kay-dăs, was commissioned by special decree of the Court of Ruler Krē-ōn and Sovereign Ă-mĭn-tă and charged with joining the elite Royal Guard of the Supreme Bloodline only leaving with the power of my life breath. My sire did this before me and my offspring will continue when I finish. May the might of the Elders aid me and may they preserve this account from the ravages of war and distortions of time.

In the First Generation of the Second Age, a great disturbance had occurred. The whole world was in civil war; the just and the fallen, the correct and the misguided. This war was both bloodthirsty and cruel. The generation that fought in it are shadows of their former selves. There are not many men and women left, apart from a few ancients that are mere husks of what they once were. The world became harsh and unforgiving.

My people have been running from our foe for a long time but it was not always so. There was a time when the bloodlines were friends with those they are now estranged from, or so the generation of my Sire claims. There are four bloodlines of my people: The Ă-kay-dăs who are charged with defence and training superb warriors, the Scy-thĕs with their making and crafting skills; the Kōr-ăx who are charged with finding food for the community and the Heir-ăxe who are in charge of our cave stores and food pits.

My people left their old home with the promise of life and new lands far from the oppressive reign of the old High King

Ēl-ō-hĭm, who kept them safe, who fed them and clothed them. He gave them everything that was good for them, but this was not enough. In their blindness and stupidity, they left him for promises of a place where they could do what they wanted. How could they be so blind to leave a ruler who loved and cared for them to follow the guides they did not know and who they were warned about? They rebelled against The High King and decided their own path. They attacked his servants who implored them to stay, seeking how they might restrain my people, to ask for forgiveness while it may still be found.

My people left with most of the men and women in the bloodlines. The Ă-kay-dăs, the heirs of Nĭk-sŭs and A-ē-tŏn, left first being the most eager to reach the new lands. The Hēir-ăxe, the heirs of Pān-thĕ-răs and Krāt-ēs, and the Kŏr-ăx, the heirs of Dŷ-măs and Zōs-ĭmē, travelled next being in the middle of our convoy. Finally, the heirs of Mĕm-nŏn and Sky-llă, the Scy-thĕs brought up the rear being slower than the other bloodlines. They brought the tents, livestock, their children and industry. They brought their old and young, their strong and weak, everyone who wanted a free life. My people searched for a new land in which to live. They travelled across the Dead Lands, suffering the scorching, burning, angry sun to travel to the new home. People died in their hundreds making this journey and all with just a promise of what the destination was. They struggled across in torment and dust. People fell for just a drink of water and there were none to pick them up or help them. Sires buried Heirs and Dames left Heiresses in graves of sand. By the time they reached the new lands, many had fallen never to rise again. My people had dwindled to only two hundred people from each bloodline, with the founder bloodline heirs acting as leaders.

My people were once a powerful and important nation. They were once beloved of the gods, but my people turned aside. They lost their path and looked away from the gods. Now they are banished with little hope of survival or reconciliation. They were led astray by their friends, who dishonoured their promise to show my people a land flowing with milk and honey. They showed them a world of pain, sorrow and ash. They then turned on my people and imprisoned them in the new lands. They lulled my people to sleep with promise of wealth and power but when my people awoke, all they had was gone.

The bloodlines had agreed early on that they needed one Ruler, especially when at war, or else each would act in self-interest. It was therefore decided to have one Supreme Ruler to guide and protect the nation. He was to be a figurehead in battle, a strategic genius and a warrior to chase our foes off our land and cast them down in submission. His woman was to be the Governor of the settlements and civilian life, she was to be our Sovereign. Her job was to monitor sicknesses, granary levels and govern the various villages and outposts. Both the Rulers were to be mouthpieces of the nation, acting as representatives and to build unity in all the different bloodlines. The Old Rulers were such people: his Heir, although young, showed the hallmarks of his noble heritage. His first task after his crowning was to appoint his Royal Guards. Their job is protecting the Ruler and his bloodline from dangers. They are to live and eat in the royal house and to guard the Supreme Ruler being loyal unto the point of death. Failure to protect the Supreme Ruler by the Royal Guard is punishable by death. They are in effect slaves to the Ruler in that they are at his every command and must do his will over theirs. Once assigned the Royal Guard swear loyalty in front of all the bloodlines. They take an oath of blood which must be honoured until death, not even the ruler can release them from this oath. They can only be released by the death of the Supreme Rulers. To find the best Royal Guards, the Ruler held noble competitions.

My people found a new place to live on the feet of the mountains. The peaks and cliffs rose above the camps; they belittled my people in their power and majesty. They often wondered what secrets their slopes held. Would they bring the bloodlines riches or sorrows? After waiting for all the bloodlines to collect, they decided to start new lives here. Crops were planted and flocks tended. Then the Elders record the coming of the enemy. They attacked a small outpost on the outskirts of the main village. It was during a morning mist, the outpost defences were poor due to the little time we had been given to develop them and were soon overrun. The inhabitants were slaughtered and the outpost sacked. The attacks on the main settlement were relentless and eventually forced all the villagers to flee for fear of their lives. The Elders had to then decide what to do; either enter the slopes of the mountains or stand and fight. There is only one memory of this time, captured by the words of our leaders. The words are passed from generation to generation, never to be forgotten, never to be changed.

> We feel bruised and broken.
> We are betrayed and forgotten.
> We feel ruined and rejected.
> We are dead and cold.
>
> We cannot enjoy the sun's warm rays.
> We cannot feel the rain's refreshing coolness.
> We cannot enjoy the joy that excites the blood.
> We cannot feel alive.
>
> How did it come to this?
> How have we fallen so far?
> How did we become so lost?
> How shall we return?
>
> They first came to us with faces of people to be trusted.
> They came to us trying to be friendly.
> They wanted to show us greatness.
> They said they were friends.
>
> They lulled us to sleep with their soft words.
> They promised us riches untold.
> They told us of sweetness and happiness.
> They slowly drew us away from the path.
>
> Their words were poison to us.
> Their riches turned to ash.
> The sweetness made us sick and ill.
> Their paths led to pain, ruin and desolation.

They turned on us when we were lost.
They were proven false.
They were not to be trusted.
They betrayed us to become our enemies.

They showed their true colours.
They became our mortal enemies.
They are dishonoured in life.
They are liars in death.

Curse them forever, and suffer them not
To let them breathe the air or pollute the land.
Plan their downfall and end their days,
Lest they contrive the end of our ways.

When my Sire was young, the Elders saw fit to move into the mountain foothills for refuge. My people's home is now a world of ice and snow. The Mighty Mountains are the crown of the world. They are fit for a Ruler as they rise tall and impressive. They have wide, ice covered faces and knife-like ridges. They have flat, snow covered plateau and steep sides. They are steep and foreboding, only the toughest can live here. The coldness slows the life breath, freezes the heart, cools the blood and makes a foolish person dead. The Elders decreed that my people would stay in the foothills. The mountains are a refuge in trouble and a prison in peace. Out of this time of testing the warriors not only became skilled but were melded together to form a fighting force. They became strong and skilled, tough and unrelenting.

My people now live on the foothills of the Mighty Mountains, in this the Third Age. To journey into the mountains is to face unknown perils and to seal their fates forever, as there must surely be fewer resources that can be used in the heart of the mountains and the weather will bite harder should my people enter the forbidding peaks. The other option is to face the hordes of darkness, but with only simple hunting weapons to defend themselves and thin, weak armour, lacking mines of ore to make more weapons. They, on the other hand, have been preparing for years. Their armies are without number; their armour is thick, their weapons sharp, their resolve and hatred of my people fixed. That was how my people were brought to their fallen condition, recorded by the stories of the Elders who lived to see it happen and who told it to their children. It is a duty to remember this and to faithfully pass it to the next generation.

My Great Grandsire, born in the first generation and living to see the worst of the civil war, survived although he was a broken man. He heard my life cries as I was born. He turned towards my cries and with the aid of my Sire felt his way over to me. He took me up in his thin frail arms assisted by my dam and lifted me up high to the heavens. With tears of sorrows in his pale blue eyes he kissed my head and whispered a message in my ear.

He said, "Heir of my flesh, I mourn that you entered this world that you had to know a fallen world such as this. I name you Āi-ās, meaning mourner, because you will see the end of all things that we knew. To you will fall the task of living with my mistakes. By my actions I have cursed you and by my failure you must suffer. I am distraught that one as tender, innocent and soft as you must live in this world. I wish I could have saved you, my young one." He is a mere shell of his old self. As the last of the old generation he is one of the sole survivors of the upheaval. His skin is tired, hanging loose on his body and is as cold as the ice of the mountains. His hair is thin and white, not like wool but like icicles and is pressed close to his skull. His face is tired and thin as a hunting spear shaft that has been worn smooth with age. His eyes are sightless and lifeless which some people say happens if you see a terrible sight. Even though the pale blues eyes have no sight, when they are turned towards you it is as if he is watching your innermost being. He is ancient and weary; time has passed him by and like the last few snow crystals of a melting, his time is fast running out. He is trapped in his mind and cannot be rid of the phantoms of the past. No sleep can help him escape; only the passing of his life breath can easy his tormented mind. He spends most of his time weeping but will refuse comfort. He weeps for the past, for what he has done and seen but mostly for what he has lost. His heir, my Grandsire died fighting in the wars.

When I was but six winters, I saw the life breath of my Great Grandsire leave him. He is burned into my memory. As he slowly grew weaker and the last of his life ebbed away he waved his hand, frantically groping for my arm. His bones were cold and frail. His skin, although not warm in life, had an unnatural coldness that made me want to pull away and I had to fight the urge. He weakly mouthed some words so that I had to move my ear right over his mouth to hear him speak in a weakened voice that was on the verge of being lost. He said, words of wisdom that I shall never forget to my dying day, "Heed my warning; the heart and neck shall kill but all else will be your undoing". With these final words he breathed out deeply and his head lolled to one side. The last of the ancient warriors was gone.

When I was ten and six, my sire taught me the two most important lessons of my life. The first lesson was the Empty Face. During the depths of winter he filled a tub of water and made me sit in the tub through the coldest part of the night. The water chilled my blood and slowed my very life. I slowly lost control of my limbs and they shivered trying desperately to function. My teeth shook and chattered until it felt as though they would fall out. My mind wandered and my skin turned pale blue through the cold. As I sat there my sire told me of war.

He instructed, "You must not show emotion or show weakness. To look strong is to be strong. Relax and let the water flow around you. Let it numb you and chill you to the bone. Allow it to strip your face of feeling and emotion. When it is empty of all indication then you have the Empty Face. Concentrate on it and remember the feeling. You must use this face when you want to show nothing." The experience nearly killed me, but it made me stronger. The second lesson was Respect. He taught me the value of a blood brother or sister; the value of friendship, loyalty and rules. I can still remember his words.

"Honour either makes or breaks a warrior. Without honour we are no more than animals fighting for survival. A man may fall, but his honour will make him immortal. When we are dead and feasting at the tables of our bloodlines we will live on the shadow of our honour. Our names will be held in infamy if we live dishonourably, but our names can live forever and outlast everything if we strive to be honourable and brave. Remember we are born with nothing and we leave with nothing, but honour governs our lives. To be honourable is to defend the weak, honour the elders, show courage, be brave and refuse to surrender. The ultimate honour is to give your life breath in battle, defending our lands and people from enemies. To gain honour is to be accepted to the tables of our ancestors, to feast with them for the rest of time. To surrender or take your own life will put your name and the names of the ones you love in infamy for eternity.

In the summer of my twenty and first year, in the First Generation of the Third Generation, the Ruler of the Bloodlines, Bă-sĭl-ēūs, died and was laid to rest in the caves of his ancestors, next to his woman Ăff-ĭă, who had died of sickness the same year. This double blow fell heavily on the hearts of our nation, especially the heir of the Throne of Power, Krē-ōn. The Bloodlines assembled in all their strength. Men dressed for war to honour their Ruler and wore black cloaks to show their grief. Women dressed in black to show their sorrow and wailed with grief to mourn the passing of the Supreme Ruler. The funeral march both celebrated the Ruler's life and mourned his death. The body is carried on the shoulders of his most loyal Royal Guards from headquarters to the resting place of his fore sires. Behind the body walks the heir. He walks with an Empty Face; blank of all emotion, unreadable and cold. Next to him stands his woman, veiled and holding his arm. A lone horn leads the procession, its mournful song echoing up the passage, amplifying the sound and resonating the notes. The bloodlines assembled along the route to wish the Ruler farewell for the final time. I remember walking behind as heir of the Captain of the Royal Guard and watching the people show their respect. Women dipping their heads and bobbing down as the body is borne past. Men fall to one knee and remain until the body has passed, faces looking at the ground. Warriors kneel, lay their spear on the ground and with head bowed place their fists on the ground in submission to the passing Ruler. I saw tears in the eyes of all and the pain that each bore. Bă-sĭl-ēūs was well loved and respected, his passing was sad and worthy of grief.

Once the procession arrives at the burial caves the horn falls silent. A voice begins to sing, it is Ă-mĭn-tă, woman of Krē-ōn. Her voice is sad and mournful. It is enough to rend a heart in two. She sings in a voice torn by grief and pain, the Death Chant of Bă-sĭl-ēūs. It tells of his life, his honour and his respect among the bloodlines. She sings louder and louder, calling on the ancestors to receive a warrior to their table. That he may sleep for eternity in peace and without dishonour. Then the song ends and all falls silent. The captain of the guard pulls aside the stone sealing the cave and the body is marched into the cave. When the body is laid in the tomb, the bearers return and form a line outside. The stone is rolled back, grating against the mouth of the cave.

The guards then turn to Krē-ōn; fall to their knees and in unison cry out "Hail Head of the Bloodline. Hail the heir of Bă-sĭl-ēūs I." Everyone follows suit, falling to one knee and the Ruler, without a word or flicker of emotion, turns to walk back to headquarters. That night there is wailing and sadness as Bă-sĭl-ēūs I is remembered and honoured.

The new day sees the oath-taking for the New Ruler. The Elders, surviving offspring of the founders of the bloodline, stand before their New Supreme Ruler to swear their loyalty and that of their bloodlines. Each man steps forward and in a loud voice proclaims the loyalty of their Bloodline.

The Elder of the Ă-kay-dăs, my bloodline, steps forward. "The Ă-kay-dăs will fight and serve you."

The Ruler replies "Give your oath to me."

The Elder replies, "We will die for you." He takes a knife from its scabbard at his side, slits his hand and repeats his oath. An oath sworn in blood can never be retracted or forgotten. All the nations declare the loyalties of their warriors to Ruler

Krē-ōn and him alone. Once all the bloodlines have sworn their allegiance the hall falls silent as the iron crown of the Nation is brought forward and placed on the Supreme Ruler's Head. My sire Stră-thōn, as head of the Royal Guard, brings the Black Spear of Command for the Ruler. He places it on the ground in front of the Ruler. This is the moment; if Krē-ōn picks up the spear we shall have a new Ruler. If he does not all is lost. The Ruler rises to take the spear, he brandishes it aloof. The attention then turns to the Ă-mĭn-tă; her white crown is brought forward and the white spear of command is laid at her feet.

Once crowned, the Ruler stands. He lifts his hands and we all fall to our knees as our Ruler addresses us for the first time. "Loyal Citizens, I am your new Ruler, elected by my sire and embraced by the Elders. Warriors, to you I say that you will fight for me, for honour and riches. Civilians, to you I say, support and help the warriors in their task; you shall receive peace to live." As the echo of his words fall silent a new noise grows and shakes the walls of the hall. The Great Horns only blown in national celebration or in alarm sound out. Their blasts race over the mountains proclaiming to the world the message. As the horn dies and the echoes fall silent, the hall breaks into cheering. Men and women, old and young all break into voice to welcome our new leader. People stamp their feet in jubilation, warriors clash shield and spear to celebrate, for hope is restored to our great nation. We have a New Ruler and our nation will survive for another generation.

CHAPTER 2

Now THE NEW Supreme Ruler has been crowned, the first official task is for him to appoint his Royal Guard. To find the best warriors Krē-ōn, Ruler of the Bloodlines seeks out the fittest and most able warriors in the traditional way of the Royal Competitions. As with every competition there are many applicants. Succeeding at the Royal Competitions not only proves one's worth in the Warrior Elite, but also the gateway to fame, honour and position. I remember my father talking about the time when he, as a gangly sun-beaten youth applied and then was successful at the competition. He served the Old Ruler up to the point of his death. I grew up in the Royal Compounds learning how to be a warrior and now I face the biggest challenge of my life. I applied to join the competitions and was readily accepted; good warriors are in short supply in our settlement as we have not seen action for some years. The men have grown lazy and weak, so the job of the recruiters to find the best warriors is hard.

I remember preparing the ground for the competition. When the Supreme Ruler decided to hold the competition on the fields of Snowy Plateau, a frantic activity of work broke out to make things ready. There were four gangs of men to work, making the accommodations, levelling the field and constructing the spectator stands. We arrived a whole moon cycle early to finish our work. My gang are in charge of making the spectator stands. Firstly we need earth and stone to build a spectator mound. The gang in charge of flattening the ground will provide us with baskets of materials needed. The stone is collected from the mountain that borders one side of the field and we need it to hold the soil mound together and prevent it from breaking down. On the first day we mark the area needed for the mound. We also send part of our gang to the rock slopes to collect loose rubble. By the afternoon we have finished and sit down waiting for our earth to arrive. We jeer at the gang working the ground for their slowness, as they labour and toil to fill the baskets for us to use. The first baskets are filled and ready to move. The gang splits into pairs to heft the heavy baskets full of mound materials. We struggle back and forth, singing as we work to keep our spirits up. As the darkness falls, we finish our work and stand back to admire the ankle deep covering of packed earth in the foundation stones. The second day dawns bright but cold and the gang arrives dressed in furs and capes to keep the warmth from the night. Fuelled by hot oat mix and warm water, we continue to work laying the earth and packing it down to prevent the foundation from sinking. One in every four men is assigned to continue work on the rock foundation, building it higher as the soil level deepens. My gang has split into different task groups, six in each. Four of these men will act as basket carriers, one will work on the rocks making the walls higher and the last man will act as an earth rammer, packing the soil down tight. My job is a stone worker, using the rock we are supplied with from the mountain. By mid-afternoon, the wall is under pressure, as the earth builds behind it. Some parts are leaking; the stones are not close enough to hold back the soil. The builders have to keep going back over the wall to refill the gaps. That night we rest in the work camps, lying around the fires to keep warm. Long into the night we talk and joke about the up-coming challenge. The foreman comes around and orders us to bed down; that finishes all conversations.

The next morning when I wake I am cold and stiff; the fire went out during the night with no one to tend it. I collect my breakfast rations, then after warming up, I continue work. Slowly the mound grows bigger and bigger as work is completed. The competition field is flattened out ready for the fighting. The tent blocks are raised and the Royal Compound is constructed.

The sounds of construction surround us; the hammering of metal on metal, the sawing of coarse timbers, the rattling of pulley systems and the dull thumps of spades on earth. The days pass with the deadline tramping nearer and nearer. The buildings grow on the horizon, bigger and bigger. The Foremen cajole and shove as they organize their charges, complete structures and monitor the progress of their tasks. Slowly but surely as the competition arrives the list of jobs becomes fewer.

The day before the competition dawns cool with a light mist. The construction work of the stands is finished and the field is flat, so both the gangs of workers prepare benches for people to sit on. Packs of roughly cut planks are brought and large hammers are used to hit in the thick nails. I and one of my far blood group members are responsible for making some of the benches. He puts the nails in place and I swing the mighty hammer. Once started he picks up his hammer and alternately hits the nail. There is much trust for him to hold the nail and for me to miss his hand. Dull hammering is heard all over the grounds with the sound of laughing and talking as the labourers anticipate the completion of this large task. The Foremen indulge us because there is little left to do. The day ends with everyone having an extra ration of oat mix, hot and soothing after the work of the day. The warmth of the food helps to restore my flesh to normal condition. The heat flows from my stomach up over my shoulders and thence to my fingers and down my legs to revitalize my toes. That night I lie under my blanket to conserve my heat. The next morning sees us knocking down the work camps to make space for the supply wagons. We rake over the fires to kill all the embers and dismantle the storage tents, loading all the tools onto the wagons for moving back to headquarters.

Suddenly, the sound of horns splits the air, announcing the arrival of the Supreme Rulers. Along with swarms of people in the camps, I run to the main causeway into the new settlement to see the arrivals. My sire is Captain of the Royal Guard and so the rest of my close blood group is among the close entourage. I cheer their arrival, then move to the place where our tents are set up to await our reunion. After a dinner of meat and oat mix, we sit by the fire talking about the competitions late into the night. Then we bed down.

On the first day I and all the competitors are gathered and paraded around the competition ground. In ranks we march around the ground ten times to show both the Supreme Bloodline and the spectators our quality. Competitors related to the old Royal Guard are placed at the head of the column. Many I do not know, but I recognize some. I see Nī-sūs of the Scy-thĕs and he dips his head in acknowledgement. I see Mĭk-tōr of the Ă-kay-dăs, who has been one of my best friends for as long as I can remember. Once the column has marched round in perfect step, we halt and face the Royal bench. My heart at this point is a battleground of excitement, nervousness and pride, ready to burst. As one, all the competitors raise their left fists in the air and roar the warrior's challenge. "We swear to fight fair, to find victory and to honour the Elders".

The second day is the test of Strength, one of the greatest virtues. It is also one of my favourite activities, along with weaponry. The official stands and reads the challenge and rules from the warrior's scroll in his parade ground voice, "The first competition is a wrestling match to demonstrate strength and technique. You will each be paired by size and ability. You must try to pin the other to the floor. The first to be pinned is dismissed and will not take any further part in these competitions. You will now be paired and you shall then begin on the sound of the horn". My opponent looks at me and grins as the pairs are announced. He sees a slow but strong warrior: he knows how to deal with that. I am a large warrior, much taller than most at over six standard foot lengths. However even though I have the strength and stamina, I am fast. The boundary line is set, the competitors are ready. I slowly stand and move into a crouch. He mirrors my moves and crouches, still with the stupid grin on his face. The horns are blown to signal the start and the competitors are focused and begin to circle.

Everything around me is ignored. I have eyes only for my foe. I edge forward and slowly start to circle. He moves round.

Both of us are on the balls of our feet and itching to start. Firstly, we have to probe each other's defences. He jabs forwards, but I do not move. He grins, thinking he has found a weakness; that I am slow. The real attack will start soon. He moves forward testing my defences again and decides that I cannot be feigning. Now he will start to attack for real. My heart beats slowly and powerfully; I am calm and controlled. My feet and legs tense ready to dodge and move; I am light and fast as the wind. My eyes are open and fixed on my prey; my judgment is not clouded and I know what I must do. With the speed of a blink he lunges. I was expecting it and time seems to slow down. Now I must show my skill. I whip to my left, turning so that now I am beside his flight path. He passes harmlessly in front of me. The look of shock and horror on his face is like sweet meat. As he falls forward trying to wrestle a foe that has outmanoeuvred him, it is my turn to attack. I lunge, grip his arm and pull myself onto his back. The game is over and time resumes its pace. The crowd is cheering and bellowing my name. My mind needs time to catch up with my actions. From deep down inside my heart there is surge of energy. I tilt my head back and let loose with the warrior's song, the long cry of victory. I am aware of the ground writhing beneath me as my pinned prey tries to wrestle me off, trying to come back into the game after he knows it is too late. I stand allowing the conquered to rise. I take his hand and with both of us grinning we embrace with a hearty back slap as comrades. There are no hard feelings for we both knew the stakes and one of us made a mistake. As my Sire says, a true warrior in the heat of battle acts, not thinks.

As we walk to the edge of the arena there are other pairs who are joining us. Some are quiet and bitter; some are recovering breath and discussing tactics; some like me are joking or talking. Once all the bouts have been decided, the competitors form two columns. One is filled with happy men who are ready for the next competition, while the other has those who were not so successful. We once again march around the grounds ten times. Then the two columns form on either side of the ground. We bow to the Royal bench, then to each other. The victor's column leaves first and then the other. After a meal with my close blood group, play wrestling with my little sibling and a quick talk with my Sire, I bed down for the night, happy with the progress and confident for tomorrow.

The third day starts, as the others, with the parade. Looking back the column is now only half as big and I start to see faces I remember from yesterday. Today will see more competitors' dreams dashed, as we run the messenger trails. An official of the court stands to set the challenge and read the rules. "All competitors hear and adhere to the rules about to be put before you. Firstly, all competitors must run the messenger trails without falling behind the following officials. Secondly, no competitor must leave the main trail. You must keep running and must navigate for yourself. All those who reach the finish line today will enter into the next level of competitions. Those who do not make it will however be considered for admission into the ranks of the heavy spearmen. Failure to comply with the rules will result in being disqualified. May the training and knowledge of the Elders guide and protect you all and lead the strongest to victory."

He bows to the Ruler and as he sits the Signal is given to start the challenge. The horns are blown and to loud cheers of encouragement, we the competitors begin to warm up. We jog round the field preparing both body and will for this gruelling challenge. Then a white horn is blown in a long low mournful note and the crowd at one corner of the field parts to reveal the entrance to the messenger trail. At once, some of the men break into a fast sprint to gain an early advantage. They speed over the competition field and race out of the grounds, running headlong down the trail. I look towards my Sire and roll my eyes. He smiles and salutes me, his left fist clenched in the air. I bow my head and then with a deep breath take a place near the middle of the jogging column, pass through the crowd and start the messenger trail.

The entrance is marked by the spear rocks; two long rock pinnacles with razor edges and jutting out tips standing either side of the mountain trail. The trail itself is narrow and windy.

As I enter, I remember the countless times I have already run here, although being in a large group will make it harder. My main concern is that if I have to overtake people it will be hard, especially if they do not want me to pass. However this is not a race; there is no first or second place, only completion or failure. I start the methodical pace I was taught as a child. Marching to us is second nature. Forced marches are familiar and long distance running simply sharpens our appetite and sleep. The tight narrow paths are hard to make out and a stumble could bring a whole line of warriors to a stop or mean the fallen man is trampled as others try to swerve out of the way. I move up, putting pressure on the racer in front to pick up the pace or move. He twists to one side to look, sees my determination and squeezes over. I slip past him like an ice floe on a river. I focus on keeping the pace constant and avoiding loose or broken ground. We come to a split in the track and I bend to the left, overtaking a runner who slows to check his direction. This is the easy part of the track. The path is smooth, a slight slope forward with no pot holes. There is little snow at this point since the gorge is fairly straight and the wind blows out the drifts that build up overnight. Suddenly there is a cry and a runner falls over, clutching his leg. Behind him there is frantic activity and shouting as men warn each other and try to avoid the fallen man. Another man falls over him after trying to jump. Many simply stop, hoping the officials have seen the incident and they will not be disqualified. Leaving the tangle of men to sort themselves out, I keep on running, easily as if I am still a boy. I lift my eyes from the track under me and look ahead. Only ten runners are in front of me now; this may not be a race, but I still want to be near the head.

After two hours on the run, the first bloodline village swings into view as we round a corner. The contestants stream into the village to cheers from the waiting spectators. We eagerly take the drinks and food provided. The competitors have become strung out and while the first to enter the village are resting and eating, others constantly stream in. There is now an option facing us. We can wait in the village and rest until just before the officials arrive or we can continue. I have a drink, something to eat, nod to the others in the group I arrived with, and then after a quick stretch, along with the more determined runners I enter the gorge again and continue the run. The sooner I finish the race the sooner I can have a proper rest.

The next leg of the track passes smoothly. The lead runner changes many times, but I am not interested in being first as long as I am in the leadership group. The story is the same at the Scy-thĕs village, after a quick drink and a bite to eat, I and the rest of the determined warriors move again. On the next stretch the track becomes harder and some begin to lose energy. I still have energy and an idea. If we are to fight beside one another then we must start working together. I slacken my pace, allowing others to pass me, working my way to the back of the leading warriors. As I jog I begin to chant; the marching songs of old; the ones used to set the pace on a long march. As I start to chant the warriors look back at me as if I am mad, wasting my energy so. Some start to slow as they are distracted by my chanting. I chant louder, urging them on. Some of the warriors catch my madness and understand my gift of help. One by one all the warriors begin to fall into the chant's pace. They begin to run in time and with new energy. Those with more breath take up the song. This is now not a race but almost a cooperative march. By aiding each other, we begin to form friendships that will seal the Royal Guard into the most powerful force in our great nation. Come mountain height or snow drift, tiredness or pain, we can conquer all, when we stand as one.

As we reach the Heir-ăxe village we pour into the encampment like a snow flood down the mountains. The spectators cheer and bellow, having waited so long to see the best of the warriors arrive. Instantly the village is a hive of activity as drinks and food are passed out. I slow to a walk and hear my name on everyone's lips. I simply bow and take a drink. As I drink, I am approached by a group of runners. One of them steps forward and bows to me. His reserved nature and slow way of thinking carefully shows he is from the Scy-thĕs. In a calm and quiet voice he begins, "On behalf of the warriors gathered, I would like to thank you for melding us as one. We would all be honoured and grateful if you would continue as our leader." After thinking carefully, I slowly nod showing my agreement to their idea. I suggest that we drink up and prepare to depart. To cheers and a few groans, we finish our drinks and move off towards the Kōr-ăx village and the end of the race.

This part of the passage should be easy; a down-hill slope and a reasonably wide path. But after having run so far, energy levels are falling and some runners find this the hardest part. As we leave the village, the people flood the passage, cheering us on. I allow myself to drop my Empty Face and grin. I take a breath and take up the song again. This time I run at the end to encourage the stragglers and I chant alone. We jog in time to the life of the song. As we run through the gorge, people line the ridge to cheer us on. This is the final stretch of the race, so we are running slower but that does not matter because the officials are far behind us. We continue to run, focussing on staying in time with the music and missing the snow patches on the path that can slip up the unwary and break up the line. Just before we regain the competition fields, we see the village of Kōr-ăx, at the bottom of the hill where the track levels out again. Upon reaching the village we do not stop, since we are so close now. We can hear the excited cheers of the spectators as they hear us approaching. We turn a corner and suddenly we can see the finish line and all the frantic spectators waving and cheering. The noise is deafening, though they are still over three hundred paces away.

I stop singing and raise my voice so all the runner can hear, "Remember my brothers, we are here to give them a sight they can never forget. Stand straight, look forward and move as one." I then begin to jog as the line of men pull back together, jogging in perfect synchrony. We do not care that we are at the end of our strength. It seems as if we have waited our entire lives to be at this place at this moment and we will savour it. To roars of the spectators, we enter the competition field. We jog in step, like a battalion perfectly moving as one. We cross the finish line and the pitch of the cheering seems to rise like the mountains behind us. Once over the line, I raise my left arm with my hand open facing upward and with perfect timing fold my hand into a fist; the signal to stop. With perfect manoeuvring and pacing the whole company slows to a walk and then a halt coming to stop directly opposite the royal bench. I lower my arm to point to the royal bench and we turn and bow.

There is cheering and celebrating that evening. I sit and eat with my close blood group around the fire, they talk and joke. After eating there is no strength left in my bones to wrestle with my little sibling and so with the help of my Sire, who walks me to my mat, I go to bed early. Since my close blood group is attached to the royal guard we are given a three room tent; One main living area with two compartments coming off the main room one on each side, which function as sleeping areas. The race is over and it is time to rest for the next challenge tomorrow.

As I turn over to face away from the breeze blowing along the floor, there is a loud cough by the main entrance to our close blood group's sleeping tent. Since the tents are made of woven cloth there is no way to announce a guest other than a loud cough, such as the one used now. I roll over and push the corner of my curtain aside to watch for the guest. My sire, Stră-thōn, looks at my dam, Chū-ră, who shrugs; no one is expected. He moves over to the tent flap and draws it aside, blocking the entrance with his body to shield the fire and sleeping area from the draught that will enter through the doorway. From my vantage point I cannot see who awaits admittance but my sire's posture, shows him ready for, it could be, unexpected company. Being a guard in the Ruler's service has made him cautious with strangers. He steps back after a moment's pause; Two people enter; his old brother in arms Nīk-ă-tōr and a fur swaddled stranger who looks around and then with grace and gentle movement walks slowly into the main compartment, head held high and shoulders back. The stranger sits and edges close to the fire to keep warm. Chū-ră sits on the left of the stranger and Stră-thōn sits to the left of his comrade Nīk-ă-tōr. Chū-ră takes the pot from the stove and fills bowls of stew for the guests. Nīk-ă-tōr and Stră-thōn are laughing and joking about the competitions, interested only in each other. Chū-ră smiles to the hooded figure, who must be shy, but seems close to Nīk-ă-tōr. Nīk-ă-tōr catches Chū-ră's eye who glances over to the stranger before looking back to Nīk-ă-tōr. He smiles and nods his head. He leans over the fire with a smile on his face, "Kă-llī-ōpē, these people are friends and mean you no harm."

With these words of comfort the stranger removes the hood and shakes out long hair that is pale as silver. It is tied back and fashioned into one single plait that runs down over the shoulder. She, for the stranger has indeed revealed herself to be a young woman, has large eyes of a pale, delicate blue. Her face is slim and finely boned. Her beauty is breath-taking and unrivalled. She nervously accepts the bowl from Chū-ră who smiles reassuringly. After a few tastes she smiles and her whole face seems to light up as she begins to eagerly eat the hot stew. After finishing her bowl, Chū-ră offers to refill it. She savours this more slowly and begins talking to Chū-ră. It seems she is the Heiress of a friend of Nīk-ă-tōr who wanted to meet the captain of the Royal Guard.

After staying for more food and a long talk with Stră-thōn and Chū-ră, both Nīk-ă-tōr and Kă-llī-ōpē stand to take their leave. Kă-llī-ōpē pulls her hood up, although she keeps it back from her face since she is comfortable with these new friends. She sweeps a loose strand of hair back behind her ear and looks down, blushing a deep crimson as Stră-thōn makes a joke. Stră-thōn then pulls back the entrance curtain and lets them out. He then releases the curtain to fall back and sits back down at the fire. I move my head off my stiff shoulder and roll back onto my sleeping mat. That was the first time I had ever seen Kă-llī-ōpē.

The third day of the Royal Competition dawns chilly; a reminder of the cold world we live in. As the competitors collect for the next challenge, I take some time to look at the faces of the warriors and the spectators. I see my sire and dam with my sibling, they wave and cheer for me. I bow and smile at them, raising my left fist in the warrior's greeting. Not too far from them sits Nīk-ă-tōr. He sees me, bows and waves. I pull myself up high with a smirk and bow my head. He laughs at my joke about his height, which is much less than mine, and shakes his head. To his left, wrapped in furs, sits Kă-llī-ōpē, watching me. I meet her eyes and then bow low, she smiles. I look back to Nīk-ă-tōr who is watching us; he smirks and his eyebrows twitch.

A horn sounds and the competitors prepare for the challenge. With a last bow to Kă-llī-ōpē and Nīk-ă-tōr, and a wave to my close blood group, I move over to the start line. Now is the time to prepare myself. I breathe slowly, savouring the smell of the sweet fresh air in my nostrils and the cooling steady draught on my skin. I slowly flex my arms, letting my muscles work and warm up. I shake my legs to keep them loose and mobile; planted legs make movement slower and lazy. I look at the cliff face and let my eye wander over the rocks, looking for a route up.

Once again the official stands to read the challenge and state the rules. "Today is the third challenge. Those who succeed will be admitted into the service of Ruler and Nation. To survive you must reach the peak of the cliffs in six chimes of the Bell. After the sixth bell any contestant not over the finish line will not be allowed into the Royal Guard. The Ruler wishes you all speed and fortune." I see one, but I must be quick to move up to my chosen spot. I only have six hours for the climb. Out of the corner of my eye, I note competitors watching me; they follow the course of my eyes, trying to see my route and to use it. I look back to the peak, wearing the Empty Face so that none can see my true thoughts. The official sits down and the horn sounds again to announce the start of the challenge. With a last look over the spectators I roar a deep bellow to build up my fighting blood. I charge bellowing and launch myself at the rock to start my climb. While I have energy I will climb fast.

The cliffs looked reasonable, even a trifle small from where I was, but as I run towards them they seem to grow higher, taller and dreadful. Soon I am climbing, never looking down. I climb as if time is chasing me and coming closer. There is a sharp ringing noise from below as the first hour sounds off. This acts like a spur, making me work harder, all the more determined to reach the pinnacle in time. I reach up to find a handhold and grasp a stone outcrop. I pull myself up but fall back as the stone breaks in my hand. Quickly I move back down to the handhold I was just using and steady myself. I breathe slowly and refocus my mind. I reach up again and find a new handhold. I test it; the rock holds firm so I pull myself up. I have now reached a wide ledge and allow myself to sit for a while and rest. I look down for the first time and see that I have made good progress. I must be at least a fifth of the way up so if I can keep going at my current rate I should reach the top with an hour to spare. I am still ahead of most of the competitors, but they are close, so I cannot rest for too long. I take a sip from the bottle that is slung across my back. The water is cool and soothing. I turn around, breath deeply and then grip the wall again; it is time to carry on.

I reach a part of the mountain that bulges out. I grip a rock point and pull myself up. I scrape my leg the pain raw, I look down and in that instant the rock comes away in my hand. I fall back scrabbling at the rock face for a hold. I claw at the stone finally managing to find a grasp. My other foot slips on the smooth rock and my arm muscles scream as they stretch under my full weight. There is a gasp from below as I swing in the breeze. My feet pedal in the air trying to reach rock, the bulge preventing me from reaching a foothold. My arms are burning, time is running out. I swing myself on the rock, gritting my teeth against the pain. Finally I find a foothold, there is a sigh from below and I rest for a moment before struggling on.

Time passes too quickly and I hear fourth chime bell. My fingers are sore from holding my weight, my nails are torn and bloody, my feet are covered in blisters and my clothes are ripped and dusty from the rock face. I am tired and every movement sends my muscles groaning, every handhold I have to concentrate on. It takes all my will-power to keep moving and cling to the rock. I look up and I realize I can see the top of the cliff. My heart skips a beat and my limbs seem to find new energy and are eager to climb. I start to speed up, climbing faster as I reach the peak. Below me the spectators are cheering as they see me nearing the top; I just focus on the climb. I would hate to fail at this point having come so far. My feet feel like they are slipping and I look down to check them. At the same time I stretch my hand up for the next grip and to make sure that if my feet do give way, I will not fall. My fingers grope for the next handhold, moving over the face of the cliff to find the best place. Nothing. I try further up the rock, still nothing. Sweat starts to bead on my face as I become anxious. I look up and break into a smile: my fingers are but two hands breadth away from the top of the cliff! I put my hand on the top and with one almighty heave I pull myself up. I lay on the ground, letting my body recover and enjoying the ground's support beneath me. I have made it.

I roll over onto my stomach and wince as the ground rubs on many small cuts from the climbing. I pull my feet up slowly and lift myself into a kneeling position. I look to my left and see the officials smile. I smile back and stand slowly. I look down the cliff edge at the competitors still coming up. The height is extraordinary, it is enough to make me dizzy and I step back a fraction just to be sure. I lift my left arm slowly and with the joy in my heart threatening to explode out of me, I yell the victor's chant. All the worry, tiredness and pain of climbing the cliff melt away as the snow in summer. I feel on top of the world. I bellow, letting my emotions flood out. From far below I hear the spectators answer me with a cheer. I hope Kă-llī-ōpē can see me and I wonder what she is thinking. Standing tall and walking slowly but stiffly I march across the finish line and then over to a bench to sit and rest.

Then I hear the fifth bell chime below me. I stand and walk back to the cliff, with every movement my muscles cry for rest, but I ignore them; they will not distract me from my task. I walk back to the cliff and kneel, waiting for a competitor to arrive. As one climbs up I see the exhaustion on his face. He sees me and his eyes light up, as he realizes how close he is. I reach down with my blistered, cut and torn hand. He reaches up and takes a firm grip. With all my might I heave him up. He feels heavier for being tired. He falls to the ground, as I did, to rest. The next competitor arrives and I help pull him up. Then I feel a touch on my shoulder and the first warrior I helped is alongside to help me. We link arms with me reaching down the cliff, the blood races to my head as I look down. I clasp the hand of the next contestant and shout encouragements. We both strain and the climber comes up. Many competitors are helped up in this way by me and my new partner and still they keep coming. Soon the cliff top is covered in men lying on the ground in various stages of recovery or helping others to recover. We are being melded into an elite brotherhood by helping and sharing what we have. We each take on different jobs. Having the longest reach and strength, I and my new friend are perfectly suited to helping the climbers up, while others are better at massaging muscles to help them recover. My partner is as tall as I but with much bigger muscles and a brute strength. He is, however, slower than me. He sees me watching him, breaks into a big friendly grin, gives me a hearty backslap and we resume our mission, looking for competitors to help. By the time the sixth bell sounds I and Kē-phās my new brother, for that is what he has become, have helped up a total of thirty warriors who are now part of the Royal Guard. I breathe deeply and enjoy success; I am in!

As the peals of the final bell die away an official stands and moves to the centre of the group. He bows low in all directions and begins, "Brave warriors, be happy and cheerful for you have succeeded. You have passed the challenges to join the Royal Guard. You may now rest and relax ready for the final test tomorrow…just as soon as you have climbed back down to the camp". He stops there, as one all the warriors shout at him, asking if he is joking. The official's face cracks into a smile and he suddenly unbends and becomes friendly, "Our Battle Masters have been working on inventive ways for you all to descend the mountain and we have perfected a method. It requires courage and just a hint of madness. To descend you shall all need one of these, we call them ice gliders." At this point he lifts up what looks like a large shield. It is made of thick iron glazed with wax to protect it from water. It has three points and a large ring fixed to it. The side with the ring is padded. The shield is not flat, so that as it lies on the ground the points do not all touch the ground. The official lets us gaze at it for a while, then continues, "I am sure you are all interested as to how it works. I will explain it in simple steps so all can understand. I shall also demonstrate for you. The glider is placed on the floor with the ring on top. You kneel on the glider just behind the ring. You place your hands on the ring like so and hang on. As you can see, when you are in position, you can tilt the glider. This gives you control. To slow down, you lean back heavily. To roll left you lean to your left. To roll right, you lean to your right. To speed up, and I am sure this is what all you youngsters will want to know, you lean forward and hunch down close to the glider. My favourite part of this whole adventure is the push off. When you are ready to glide we shall push you off with this." He holds up a long handled spear with a flat head. "We use these to start you off. You will not be sliding down the hillside however. Oh no! To make it easy for you and to prevent any of you falling off, we have constructed a slipway for you. It will guide the glider and all you have to do is lean with the glider and brake when you see the red flag at the bottom of the cliff. This concludes the training. When you are ready to descend, please go to my assistant. If you have any queries come to ask me."

After he has finished he turns to talk to his assistant. I cast a look at Kē-phās who nods and pushes his way forward. Unwilling to let him go first and snatch the glory, I leap over a warrior resting after his climb, and race forward to the assistant. Kē-phās flashes his teeth in a smile and also races forward, only to reach them after me. The assistant rolls his eyes but smiles. He turns to his stack of ice gliders and calls for me to help him. I eagerly lift my end of the glider and place it on the ground near the slipway. As soon as my end is down, I climb aboard and grip the ring. My hair prickles and I shiver; from excitement or fear I cannot tell. I look back over my shoulder to see the assistant arm himself with the long rod and place it near the glider, ready to push me off. Kē-phās is watching, arms crossed but smiling. "See you at the bottom, but you had better be quick or I shall catch you." He calls. I make a face at him and then look forward as the assistant grunts and the glider begins to edge forward. Closer and closer to the lip of the slipway the glider groans as it scrapes over a stone and makes me jump. Behind me I hear Kē-phās snigger to see me jump. I grit my teeth and hold on grimly. I reach the top of the lip and stop as the assistant makes the final preparation. I hear a scout horn sound a low note, warning of my imminent descent. Down the slope I can hear other scout horns passing on the message, eventually to arrive at the foot of the slipway. I turn as the assistant gives the final piece of advice. "Remember to brake when you see the red flag. Do not worry you shall see it in good time. May the Elders protect you." And with that final farewell he once again pushes the pole to the glider and braces ready to heave me forward. He grunts and gives an almighty shove. With a whisper and a gentle tilt I tip over the lip of the slipway and I am off.

The glider rapidly picks up speed as it slides down the slope. The wind rushes past me, forcing my eyes closed apart from a narrow slit. Faster and faster I race, the wind roaring in my ears. I skid round the corners, the wind whipping across my face, nearly threatening to push me off the glider. I make sure I lean with the glider as I fly over the snow. I pass a warrior who smiles and blows a note on his horn so that everyone can keep an eye on my progress. The slipway is smooth and ice covered, making the glider move all the faster. I am gripping the ring as hard as I can, but I can feel my hold wearing out as the wind and cold numb my fingers. The glider is racing down the slipway, hissing as it cuts through the snow. Either side of me the banks of snow speed past, and my grip tires. With grim determination I hold on. If I should fall off now, I will surely break something, or the next glider may even kill me. This new thought gives me the determination to hold on. I also make sure my knees are gripping the glider as best as they can. I begin to enjoy the new mode of transport.

As I follow the spine of the hills, I approach the end of the run. I follow the slipway as it gracefully swings round, eventually to arrive in the open part of the tournament ground. The last part flattens out. As I sweep round, I see the red flag and the tops of the bandstand swinging into view. I brake gently, worried that if I brake too hard my glider may overturn. However, I brake too lightly and by the time I reach the red flag with the tournament ground looming in front, I am travelling too fast and in danger of crashing. Warriors run towards me, urging me to brake; I shout at them to move away to let me bring the glider back under control. I decide on a risky manoeuvre to slow it down. The ground is level now, so I very carefully shift my position so that I am crouching rather than kneeling. Then slowly, but aware of the grounds looming ahead of me, I raise myself to stand on the glider, using my weight on the back to brake it. As I brace for impact, the glider answers and with much groaning and shuddering it slows to a stop with paces to spare until the point would have struck the benches. I breathe deeply and with weak knees step off the glider. I become aware of the spectators roaring and cheering at such an entrance. I bow and then clear the slip way as the horns sound to warn of the next glider's approach. I walk to one side where the warriors are collecting ready to help the next entry.

With an almighty bellow and grinding Kē-phās comes sliding into the arena. He also travels too fast and instead of stopping in time like me, he in an effort to avoid the benches careers past them and slips into the space between them. The warriors run after him and silence falls over the grounds as they wait to see if Kē-phās is injured. I run after them, eager to help. By the time I arrive he is on his feet, although looking dazed and confused. And no wonder for he was stopped by a left over pile of soil and rubble. The glider lies dented and bent from the collision; Kē-phās is lucky to escape without injury. I push past the warriors to him and he gives me a grin. "I am well. I have a head like a stone." He smiles, tapping his head and grimaces as he hits a bruise. I emerge with him and the arena breaks into cheering as Kē-phās takes his bow. I let him have his moment of glory before I take him to see the blood group, who welcome him; a friend of mine is a friend of theirs.

At the end of the day, with the rest of the gliders arriving without major incident and the third challenge completed, the horns sound to call the arena to order. The Royal Guard has been formed. The official stands up and breathes in deeply. "The Royal Competition finishes with the election of the Royal Guard. The final tally of guards is thirty, who must swear allegiance to the Supreme Bloodline. The oath taking ceremony will be held in two days at the tenth bell. Tomorrow are the trials to find the captain among you. Warriors, to you I say, go home and be happy. I salute you all." At this point he stiffens and performs a perfect salute. His left arm smoothly and like a well-oiled pulley, rises and clenches finishing the salute. A horn sounds and we are dismissed until the next morning.

The day of the trials for captain dawns cool but bright. After talking late into the night with my blood group, reliving the excitement of the past few days, I wake to find that my sire has carried me to bed as he did when I was a child. My dam has tucked me in so I will not feel the chill, not willing to let her child leave her care. Here in this close blood group have I found true love and I hope to have a close blood group as warm and as loving when I grow older. I fear to be alone when my life breath leaves me; but it is time to prepare. I rise and step over my sibling, pulling his blanket firmly around him to keep him warm. I rouse the fire from the embers left from the previous day. Feeding it with tinder, then with charcoal, building it back up to heat. I fill a bowl with water ready to boil for use at breakfast. Sitting on the heating stones beside the fire to warm myself and help my muscles wake and prepare for the day.

I then go to my heavy spear in the rack where it is placed next to my father's. I take the oiling rag from the bowl of goat wax and rub the shaft to protect it from the damp and to make it smooth to hold. I am careful not to over-wax or my grip will be uncertain. I then begin to wax the blade, making it smooth so that it does not catch on clothing or snag on flesh. After the blade is waxed, it must be sharpened. I take a whetstone and with long, gentle movement I hone the blade slowly and carefully making it sharper and sharper until it will cut with just a whisper. I am so focused on my work, that I do not notice my dam come out from the other sleeping section. She smiles at my concentration and leaves to fetch the close blood group's ration of water, grain and meat for breakfast. My sire comes out of the sleeping section and takes up his spear to make it ready. I learnt my skill from him, watching him every morning. I finish my spear and take up my armour. My close blood group, being of the Royal Guard, have access to metal armour, which is rare among our people. We have very poor sources of metal to work and our flocks are too few to use to make leather armour. Most warriors have to rely on their good fortune and speed to avoid injury. I have my own suit of armour that I have been fighting with and practising in. A breast plate, arm and hand gauntlets, a helmet with a faceguard and a shield as well as a dagger for close quarter work, although I will not need the dagger today. I will only need breastplate, helmet and heavy war spear.

I am so focused on my armour that I do not notice the movement behind me, or the main entrance curtain swept aside as my mother returns, and the hooded figure that enters with her. My sire stands and bows to welcome our guest. My dam speaks with a smile, "I found this poor little child wandering and asked her to join us for breakfast." My sire speaks with a warm grin, "We can always find food for one more mouth; that is, if we are faster than Āi-ās!" At the sound of my name it is as if a spell is broken, I blink and look around me. I see the robed figure and dip my head as my heart jumps. Under the hood spills long, silver hair and as the hood is tilted back the face becomes visible. The pale blue eyes inspect me and seem to fix my attention but I cannot read them. I start to breathe faster, my palms become sweaty and my heart seems to beat in my ears. Kă-llī-ōpē smiles and my courage seems to forsake me. I am tongue tied and cannot say anything, though eventually I am able to greet our guest. She gives a timid bow to me in greeting, although she seems as nervous as I. My sire nudges my dam, who has been making breakfast. They both give each other a knowing look and a smile, then with a quick cough return to their jobs. My dam calls Kă-llī-ōpē over and asks her to help with the meal. My sire walks behind me and gives me a nudge. I turn to face him and he smiles looking towards where

Kă-llī-ōpē is now helping to make hot grain mix. They seem to be talking and having a nice time. They are both smiling and now Kă-llī-ōpē laughs and suddenly my heart seems to stop dead. She is beautiful, words cannot describe her and they are too crude to attempt it.

After breakfast, the sound of the horns beckon the contestants to the final challenge of skill with weaponry to test for our captain. I heft my spear and put my armour on; I look like a warrior. I march to the competition field with my father, who is also in full armour. I march behind to show respect, as the man of the house always leads. We march in perfect synchrony, mirroring each other. At the arena my father stops and turns to the side and joins my close blood group near the royal bench to watch my performance. I march to my allotted spot. I plant my spear, spread my feet and wait. I freeze as a statue as I have been taught. I have been trained to stand with an Empty Face, not showing emotion or fear. As the rest of the competitors arrive, I see the two stances of fighting that warriors adopt. There is the fast, loose "Wind" and the slow, solid "Mountain". I fight in the 'Mountain way', using the heavy hunting spear as well as the heavy metal armour. This method uses one hit to kill and is the most protected way of fighting. Warriors who are slower use it, because they have not the speed required for the other method of fighting. I see a warrior of the Scy-thĕs who is dressed for the 'Wind' fighting stance. He wears light leather armour that will not stop direct blows; his speed will be his defence. Heavy armour would slow him down. He carries a bundle of light spears that are slung over his shoulder to replace ones that break or in times of war to throw. The way to succeed is to stay light and bleed the target to death. Warriors who are fast and agile use this method as they dislike the constriction of the heavy armour. I see Kē-phās who is dressed as a Mountain warrior. He wears heavy armour and hefts a heavy spear which looks like a twig in his hands. He sees me and grins, bowing low. I smile and return the bow, then pull myself back into my statue stance. He takes his place to the left of me and adopts an easy stance. We both wait for the rest of the warriors to appear.

There are fifteen Wind warriors and fifteen Mountain warriors. I remember what my father has taught me. The Wind warrior is more exposed to blows, but is harder to catch. The mountain warrior is less vulnerable, but cannot run. Power is needed to beat speed and speed must be beaten by power. Today will need all my skill and endurance as I have many single combats to fight and I must not be wounded.

The horns sounds and the competitors form a hollow square. In this formation any warrior can challenge any other warrior. As the competitors must fight all the other contestants it does not matter who battles first. There can only be a maximum of four fights at a time, since there are only four Battle Masters that act as judges, one from each bloodline. The competitors begin to chant and bellow as we start our blood racing. A Wind warrior steps forward and, using his spear as a pointer, challenges another Wind warrior. He bellows and rattles his spear. His opponent steps forward and falls into a warrior's stance. He crouches low, his spear raised to strike; he stands on the balls of his feet to move quickly. As is the custom, all the warriors watch the first fight before other fights begin. The two warriors move closer as the lighter wind spears are shorter than the heavy mountain ones. The spears are raised and the Battle Master raises his spear to indicate the start. The challenger runs forward to test the defence. He stabs again and again in a flurry of spear points. The defender calmly deflects them all waiting for a gap and then starts his own attack, but rather than unleashing a frantic stabbing, twirls his spear shaft like a walking staff, driving the challenger back, trying to pin him against the boundaries. The challenger smiles and drops flat, rolling to the left while the defender stabs into the dirt where the challenger was standing. The challenger jumps back to his feet and resumes his stance. The defender turns to meet him and thrusts, the challenger turns to the side and the spear goes past him. He grins and strikes the arm, causing a cut. The Battle Master raises his spear high and slams it down between the competitors to stop them competing, declaring the end of the fight. The challenger cheers and returns to his place slamming his spear butt into the ground. The defender resumes his position and assumes the Empty Face. The crowds burst into cheering and suddenly everything starts moving as the challenges are issued left, right and centre. Four challenged fights begin. There is no time to watch them all so I concentrate on reading my opponents. Those that have not perfected the Empty Face are easy to read; I see fear, excitement, nervousness and confidence.

Without warning, I hear a roar as a mountain warrior walks slowly forward into the middle of the square. He thrusts his spear forward and I smile; He has challenges me. I raise my spear butt from the ground and heft my shield. I step forward, fill my chest and accept his challenge with a long bellow. My acceptance is so powerful, that some of the fighters pull apart to look at me. I walk forward to the hollow square. Mountain against mountain, this is a fight of strength and power. I step forward and fall into my fighting stance. My shield comes to my chin; my left hand holds the spear and grips the shaft firmly. My helmet visor is pulled down and I am ready for battle. I settle and spread my feet preparing to fight. The Battle Master raises his spear and the fight is ready to begin. We begin to circle, looking for weaknesses in defences. Our spears are so close the tips nearly touch. I thrust mine forward to tap his and he jumps back. I step back to have space to manoeuvre. I stab to the left of the challenger; he moves right and forces my spear back using his shaft. I smile inwardly; I know how to pass him. I step back and turn my spear against my body. This is going to be risky, but what is the pleasure or honour an easy fight? I move forward and he thrusts his spear at me. I quickly raise my spear underneath his and push it up. He cannot stop me and I slide the shaft of my spear under his, right down his spear to his hand. I then pull it back, using the edge of the spear to cut his wrist. The Battle Master raises his spear and pushes us apart; the battle is over. The challenger cannot believe it; he looks at me in shock. I turn, heft my spear and return to my space in the square. I stop, spin round and ground my spear. I await my next challenge. As the day wears on more challenges arrive and I fight with honour and skill.

Most of the fights I cannot remember. I do remember the fight with Kē-phās though. I never challenged, letting my foes reveal themselves to me. With a large bellow Kē-phās walks towards me, he does not smile but pulls the face mask down on his helmet to hide his face. We are both warriors and we shall act as such. The Battle Master checks we are both ready for the fight, raises his spear then steps quickly back. He does not want to be in the way of these fighters. This will be a battle of strength and endurance. We both move to the crouch to prepare for battle. The cheering reaches a pinnacle as the crowd realizes the importance of this fight. I decide to draw this fight out as I want to learn all I can of this warrior. This is one of the best opportunities to learn about his fighting style. We begin the warrior dance, moving left, moving right, darting forward and dodging back. This may be fighting like a mountain but we are both equal and we need to wear each other down. For a time, we dart and dodge each other, circling around and around. The cheering is a constant background noise, heightening when either of us makes a move. I thrust forward and he knocks my spear point aside on his shield. He thrusts and I deflect the point on my shield. Because we are still moving forward, we crash shields with our spear points aside making them useless. This is now a pushing match; shield on shield.

We barge and struggle, shunt and bump. I let him push me, trying to block him, so that he will wear himself out but his strength is immense. It is like trying to hold back a snow flood with a wooden board. My foothold begins to fail and I start to slide back. Instead of holding my ground, I will have to attack. The best form of defence is attack, my sire always tells me. I start to push and walk, forcing my way forward. He is not expecting this and loses his concentration. I hit with my shield and force us apart, pulling my spear back, ready to attack. We are back to where we began and both breathing heavily; shields up, spears forward and chins on shield rims. I decide on a course of action and charge in a whirl of hits and lunges. He calmly gives ground, driving them away and deflecting the point. I keep attacking, spinning the spear, mainly using the spear butt and shaft, keeping the point in reserve. The blows are relentless and calculated. Kē-phās is still moving backward and has lost some of his confidence. I see him look left and right, trying to work out my plan. I keep hitting his shield and armour, renewing my efforts. I then start to shift my aim to his legs; he automatically drops his shield to cover the legs. I continue to hit him. Earlier I noticed a gap near his neck line when I was watching him and I use my constant hitting to move his shield away from his neck to reveal the weak spot. I judge it time to change tactics. I reverse my spear and nick him in the top of the shoulder at the base of the neck. A risky move but necessary. The crowd falls silent as Kē-phās breaks off and steps back we both bow and return to our spaces. The crowd bursts into cheers as the Battle Master raises his spear to end the match and declare the winner. As I return to my space I raise my face mask to wipe my face clear of the sweat that has formed. Kē-phās does the same and allows his face to drop into a grin.

That night, the sound of laughter and celebration is heard all over the camp as the thirty warriors celebrate and anticipate their new lives. The excitement is hanging in the air so thick you could cut it with a knife. All my blood group and close friends gather in our group's tent. Fortunately, our close blood group's tent has been placed near to other related blood groups, so by removing some tent flaps and walls, as well as clearing away clothes and bedding we can create one large walkthrough tent. One by one, blood group members and friends arrive, gathering to celebrate not only the competing in the championships but also me reaching my twenty first winter and being recognized as a man. My sire is sitting opposite me. He has not declared his pride of me in words, but I can read it in his face. His eye glitters with pride, happiness and relief. My dam is crying with joy and insists on hugging me every few minutes to show her happiness. Friends and blood group members are all singing my success and I receive their happiness. My sibling launches himself at me, squealing with joy as I catch him and let him wrestle me to the ground. He then shouts that he has beaten the great warrior and proclaims himself as the greatest warrior in the world. He is only ten and four winters and we are close friends.

A few late comers arrive at the party. Nīk-ă-tōr arrives and with him, wrapped in her furs but with her hood down showing her lovely hair, is Kă-llī-ōpē. My words stick in my throat when she arrives. My cousin sees me stutter and laughs. "Has the great warrior in the nation, the one who fought battles unscratched, been knocked senseless by a woman? This woman must be a sorcerer to make courage forsake this warrior." I give him a playful punch, he laughs and I decide to teach him a lesson. I launch myself at him and it descends into a wrestling match. Everyone shrieks and moves out of the way as my cousin and I roll across the floor. He is laughing too much to form an effective defence. Meanwhile my other cousins have been introduced to Kă-llī-ōpē and are making friends with her. She asks where the warrior is and they point me out as one of the forms rolling around on the floor. She laughs and I overhear her say, "He does not seem to have had enough of fighting so he must start again." Her voice sounds like a bird singing, like a melody, like happiness and peace. The wrestling match finishes with me sitting on my cousin's head and him admitting I am the better fighter...which I already know.

The evening passes well enough, but with no spoken contact between Kă-llī-ōpē and me. However, that does not stop me from stealing glances at her, and at various points I am sure she was glancing at me. I quickly look away, like a child caught in the act of mischief. I turn back to my cousin and continue to joke around. My sibling jumps on me and I slide him onto my knees, tickling him and smiling at his shrieks of delight. I tickle him again until he has tears of laughter in his eyes. He begs for mercy and I relent, tapping him on the palm of his upturned hand, accepting his sign of submission. In the distance I hear the chime of the bell signalling the middle of the night watch. My sire stands bidding all to be quiet with out-stretched arms, as he wishes to say something.

He smiles and with a voice tight with pride begins, "Today our bloodline has shown our worth as warriors and men. Our bloodline is known for three things. The beauty of our women (at which all the women clap), the strength of our warriors (at which all the men bellow) and the courage of our young bloods (to which all the heirs cheer). My heir has continued in the steps of his sire and grandsire of giving his oath to the ruler. My firstborn has proved his worth and skill in competing in the championships and surviving the final round. Today we celebrate this battle and the spoils of victory. Tonight we eat, we drink and we shall be merry." Amidst loud cheers he bows and resumes his seat, letting everyone continue their conversations and eating. The official part of the evening is over and the hubbub increases to a healthy hum as conversations strike up. The rest of the evening passes fast as I talk to cousins and other people at the party. I also continue to take glances out of the corner of my eye at Kă-llī-ōpē. However, my mind is tinged with sadness: this will be my last night at home with my close blood group for a long time. As eldest, I am the first to leave. To leave my close blood group fills me with fear and excitement. To leave is to accept the role of manhood, but also to face a world unknown. I have to trust that whatever power has kept me safe will continue to smile on me.

The final ceremonies of the competition are greeted by a cool, misty morning. The air is chilly and refreshing, like a new life with the promise of new beginnings. The spectator benches are filling for the final time, but instead of the loud banter of the previous day a quiet, solemn mood enshrouds the arena. Today the survivors of the Royal Competitions will forfeit their independence to become servants and slaves to the Ruler and his Close blood group. They will be awarded the most prestigious rank, the chance for great glory and riches, the chance for adventure and a comfortable life, but they will pay a dear price for such riches. The price for such a reward is to become slaves to the Ruler's will and desires. The Royal Guard have no independent thought or choice, their only option is to obey with unquestioning loyalty. The spectator benches are alive with the low hum of conversation but as the great Chime Bell marks the tenth hour of the day, the silence of expectation falls and the spectators settle in their places. Apart from a single muffled cough the arena is surrounded by silence. Then the horns break out in song as the Old Royal Guard march into the field with the Supreme Ruler in full ceremonial dress. In perfect precision and drill, the Royal Guards perform faultless manoeuvres as they escort the new Ruler to His place. At the head of the column walks Stră-thōn as captain of the guard. As they halt with perfect timing it is the new guards who must now arrive. Under the command of the Royal Battle Master we march into the ground. We carry no weapons or armour but are simply dressed in white woollen shirts and woollen trousers bound at the ankles. The Old Guard have formed to the left of the Royal Bench where the Supreme Ruler is now seated. We march into the ground and form a single column of men to the right of the Royal Bench and turn to face the old Guard.

There is not a sound on the arena except for the flapping of the banners of the Supreme Bloodline. Then the official stands to begin the proceedings. "Today the Old Guard is released from their oath of service and the New Guard take their oath of service. At the beginning of this moon cycle there were ninety warriors who thought themselves equal to the task. You see before you the strongest warriors, the survivors. They have been tested for strength and wisdom, courage and endurance and skill of arms. I present to you the New Guard. The honour of protecting the Supreme Ruler falls to the following warriors." At this point with a flourish he opens a scroll on which the names of the new guard are written. As the list is read each warrior acknowledges his name. Some raise their weapons high, other roar their defiance, some bow, but all will be remembered for this is our day. My name is at the end of the list and I concentrate to learn the names of my new comrades. The official's voice calls me back from my thoughts. "I present you with the New Royal Guards. As reward for winning the Challenge of Arms, Āi-ās, Heir of Stră-thōn, Son of the Ă-kay-dăs will command the Royal Guard." I step forward and kick the spear handle so that it spins to an overhand grip, I present it and rap it against my shield, before returning to crisp salute.

At this point a wonderful event begins. The two guards face each other, I stand opposite my father. With crisp movement and precise drill, we march towards each other in a slow proud march. When we reach each other we stop. My father with an Empty Face hands me the spear of command. I grasp the wooden shaft, feeling the smoothness, age and power of the weapon. My father steps two paces back and bows to me. The rest of the Old Guard follow suit presenting their ceremonial spears to the New Guard. They then step back and bow to the New Guard. I spin on my heel to face the Supreme Ruler and bow with the spear outstretched, near the ground. The Supreme Ruler, Krē-ōn, stands and walks to me, I see his shoes stop in front of me as he leans down and raises me up to show his acceptance of the New Guard. His eyes are blue and seem void of expression, except for a small sparkle he has always shared with me, his friend of childhood. He is indeed a warrior fit to chase our foes out of our lands. He looks me over assessing his new captain of the Royal Guard and with a nod to the old captain accepts the new Royal Guard. Now the oath taking can begin.

The Supreme Ruler holds his arm out for me to take a grip of it to swear my oath. In a deep voice he begins the solemn oath "Āi-ās, Heir of Stră-thōn, of the Bloodline Ă-kay-dăs, do you by the breath of your life, forever swear loyalty to the Supreme Ruler, until either my breath departs me or you have spent every drop of your blood? Are you willing to forsake your freedom to be bound to my will and desire? If you are a true warrior, you will embrace this honour and be prepared to die for your Ruler! Give your answer and bind yourself to my household." My answer needs no consideration. I take the small dagger proffered by the official, standing to the left of the Supreme Ruler. I lay the blade on my upturned palm, feeling the cold iron on my skin. My allegiance is sealed to the blood group of the Ruler and to be sealed with my blood. Calmly and slowly, I give my oath "I, Heir of Stră-thōn, Son of the Ă-kay-dăs, pledge life and spear to you."

He looks at me, "Swear it to me." I raise my hand with the blade in my right poised over the left. I draw the blade across the skin, scoring it and drawing blood. I extend my hand and fall to one knee proffering my blood. The official takes a cloth and collects the blood falling from my hand. Every warrior will pledge and add his blood to the cloth as proof of his allegiance. The Supreme Ruler looks at me and nods, accepting my oath. I stand and walk backwards to my place at the head of the New Guards. As I walk back past the official he gives me a white stone tablet attached to a leather lace. On it is carved my name and my promise. I hang it around my neck. This is my official seal showing my position in the Royal Guard. One by one the rest of the guard follow my example until the bowl is filled with the blood of thirty warriors. We all will carry the scar on our left hands for the rest of our lives, to remind us of our oaths. Once the oaths are complete and the final warrior resumes his place in the line, the Supreme Ruler sits, throwing his cape around his shoulders to keep himself warm against the chill. The crowds burst into cheers as the cloth of blood is held aloft showing the proof of the oaths.

The New Guard forms at the foot of the platform, ready to protect the Supreme Bloodline as they are escorted back to the Supreme Compound. The line of guards' bends and folds to form a hollow square. I take up my place at the front of the square, standing just in front of where the Supreme Bloodline will stand. The Supreme Ruler moves to his woman and offers his arm to her, in true, honourable behaviour. The delicate Supreme Sovereign takes the arm offered, stands and clings to the Supreme Ruler for support. Being still young there are no offspring yet to this union, but today the Supreme Sovereign is paler in colour than normal and wearing looser clothes. It could be a simple chill rather than big changes afoot. It is not for me to comment, only to guard and care. The Rulers descend from the platform and enter the protection square. The square seals to enclose the Supreme Bloodline and I raise my spear and thrust it forward, giving the command to move forward. Moving in perfect synchrony we march to the Supreme Compound. The excited crowds stream out of the benches and gather around the new guard. Most know better than to approach within the four pace mark of the outside of the square, but some youngsters challenge the safe zone and are met with spear rattling to push them back to a safe distance. It is not that we do not trust them, but if a Ruler was to be attacked it would be most dishonourable. As we march, I observe all the people near the square. My job is to watch for possible problems, to anticipate the crowds and see the unseen. I keep looking, not wanting to make a mistake. The march is usually only a short one, but with all the pressure of the people it takes much longer than normal. But the Supreme Rulers seem relaxed at the slowness. They are content to nod to nobles, smile at each other and accept the press of people. They have only recently bound their lives together and they are still very much in love. There is something new, they usually show their love of their people, but today is different. They are content to talk with each other. As the Compound approaches, I find myself looking more at the Rulers and less at the path, the crowds melt away and most of the guards relax. The first guard is always the most nervous.

As we approach the Royal Compound a lump forms in my throat. My close bloodline has collected at the entrance to the compound along with those close to the other guards. I make an extra effort to stand straight and look the part of Captain to the Royal Guard. My sire is there with my sibling on his shoulders and my dam at his side. All are smiling although my dam has tears in her eyes. I see the pride sparkling in my sire's eyes as he sees my progress. Next to them I see Nīk-ă-tōr and slightly bow my head to which he nods and smiles. Beside him wrapped in her furs is Kă-llī-ōpē. I instantly pull myself up tall to show my stature. I nod to her and she smiles at me. Her checks blush to a red glow as Nīk-ă-tōr nudges her, she drops her gaze and I look elsewhere. As the compound looms closer I can see the compound staff all turned out ready to great the Rulers and New Guard. The crowds by the stockade are growing as the people accompanying the squares move forward to acquire a place to see the Rulers and the New Guard. The mumbles of the crowd build into a hubbub as they welcome the arrivals. We all stand to attention and amidst the cheers of the crowds, march into the compound. As the final face of the square walks into the compound the wall sentries put their shoulders to the gate and heave with all their might. With creaks and groans the gates swing shut and the whole guard visibly relax; the first escort mission is complete.

That night there is a feast for both the new and old Royal Guards as they share this last moment together. The feast is not elaborate but it is time to talk, joke and enjoy friendship. There are rolls of smoked meat, rare oat bread baked on stones and fresh cold water, all in generous quantities. If we are to be Royal Guards we must be fit and have the strength to fight. At the head of the table sit the Supreme Rulers, the new guards sit on one side of the table and the old sit on the other.

I take great delight in introducing the new guard. "The warriors Ĭă-rĕt and Nă-ŏs from the bloodline of Heir-ăxe; these sibling heirs are known for their ability to mirror each other and to store food and protect resources. The warrior siblings Ty-phōn and Tō-bĭt, from the bloodline of Kōr-ăx; known as masters of procuring provisions and resources, although it is best not to ask where from (at which point everyone laughs). The warriors Rhă-mă and Py-thă, from the bloodline of Kōr-ăx; both skilled in the art of food preparation, with skills good enough to make a feast for a Ruler, which is just as well. (There are numerous cheers at this point). The warriors Pān-thĕ-răs and Nĭk-ōm-ēdēs, from the bloodline of Scy-thĕs; they are skilled scouts having strong endurance to travel vast distances and with good memories to re-trace routes. The warriors Nō-ē and Hy-pă-tōs, from the bloodline of the Scy-thĕs; skilled craftsmen able to make quality weapons and armour, they are also skilled inventors anticipating new ideas for the Supreme Ruler. The twin heirs Yă-nnī and Yĭ-ăn-nī, from the bloodline of Scy-thĕs; skilled hunters able to find and track prey with ease. The warriors Kăd-mŏs and Ĭă-sōn from the bloodline of the Scy-thĕs; renowned for their inventions. The governor warriors Ăb-răx, Kār-pōs, Ăt-rēŭs and Nlē-mēs from the Ă-kay-dăs' bloodline; educated and wise men, well equipped to guide the settlements. The warriors Bă-răck, A-ē-tŏn, Mīn-ō-ăs, and Kēy-x from the bloodline of the Ă-kay-dăs; master constructors, able to engineer and build using various tools and materials. The warriors Bĭ-ōn, Hy-mēn and Kē-phās from the bloodline of the Ă-kay-dăs; they will be perfect drillmasters. Finally, the warriors Ăm-ŏn, Bēn-ēdĭc-tăn, Dră-kŏn and Hē-bēr from the bloodline of Ă-kay-dăs; tactical advisors who will travel with warriors to support in battle.

The rest of the night passes with humour, conversation and a final piece of advice to the new guards from the old veterans. My sire stands up to deliver this tradition. "Be constantly aware of everything; every detail, every movement and every change. When things are most quiet and silent, that is the time for you to be alert and wary. Never let your guard down for a moment, it is better to be over-alert than to pay with your life breath for failure. Other than that enjoy life, for today we eat but tomorrow we may die." With that sobering thought in mind the feast breaks up. We all stand as the Supreme Rulers leave and then the old guard followed by the new. The new guard walk the old guard down to the stockade gate. There is solemnity as the old guard leaves to begin a new chapter in their lives. My sire is the last man out of the gate. Just before he passes through he turns around and with a tear in his eye as he watches part of his life finish, he walks towards me and embraces me. This is the last time I shall see him for a long time, as my old life falls asleep and my new life awakes. We do not speak, not trusting ourselves. We shake hands and salute each other. Then he turns around and walks away. On the rise not far from the gate I see my sibling and dam, my sire walks to them and they all turn to look and wave to me. Before me, I see my old world and happiness.

That night after a wash and supper, I bed down in the barracks where the Royal Guard stays when not on duty. Along with the other guards, we remain close to our Ruler, within calling distance should the need arise. The night is cool, a light mist flows down the mountains and envelopes the arena. Unbeknown to anyone living, evil stirs.

CHAPTER 3

In the morning, the guards assemble at dawn to receive the instructions for the day. The mist continues to swirl around, even thicker than the night. The Supreme Ruler steps out from the night quarters and stands before us to issue his orders. "Today is an easy day. We must return to Headquarters where you will begin your new lives. The Supreme Entourage and Escort will leave early as we aim to reach our destination before nightfall. Pack up your things and be ready to leave by the ninth bell". We move back to our sleeping quarters to pack our clothes, weapons and armour. Once packed I put my kit in the growing pile of equipment for transporting by the wagons. I join Kē-phās and the other guards who are arming themselves. As before I take my spear and oil it, taking care to make it ready. Hopefully I will not need it for anything more than a support for the tougher tracks. I put on my coat of rings; I must see the armourer some time to repair some damaged rings. I clamp my leg guards on, taking care to make the fittings tight and secure. I fasten on my breastplate making sure the latches are secure. My helmet onto my head and tie the straps tightly under my chin. I push my right arm into the shield loops to keep it secure and tighten the belts. Finally I grasp the spear in my left hand. I am dressed for duty.

At nine bells precisely, as the peal dies away, the Supreme Rulers quit their rooms dressed in plain travelling clothes. The Sovereign is helped into the wagon by a companion and watched by the Ruler who comes over to help when the Sovereign seems to slip. There is something wrong with her and the Companion moves back with head bowed as the Ruler takes her place. The Sovereign smiles and clings to him for support. They both slowly and carefully enter the carriage; the companion follows them in and draws the curtain across the back. She then appears on the driver's bench and sits next to the grizzled veteran driver, who pulls the horn that hangs rounds his neck and gives a quick blow. The wagon haulers, all strong young men rippling with muscles take up their pulling ropes. With a grunt, a heave and grim determination they strain. The wheels groan, the axles squeal and the wagon begins to roll slowly forward. The royal guard form up. Kē-phās, myself and another warrior march at the front, the twins warriors follow behind and the rest of the guard form on either side. We are the first to leave the arena and after us, the convoy starts to roll and begins the long march back to headquarters.

The journey is a tense and exhausting one. The mists swirl around clouding the eyes and making it hard to see. We have to rely on our hearing; each sound must be checked and identified. Suspicious sounds need to be looked for and normal ones understood. The eyes cannot be lied to but the hearing can be fooled. I hear the breathing of my men, the muffled laughter from the covered wagon, the crunch of hard ice under marching feet, the rumble of the wheels and the murmur of conversation from the driver and companion. I smell the freshness of the air, the mystery of the mists, the sweat of the wagon haulers and the oil on my spear. I see the mists wrapping around everything, the half hidden darker shapes and the nervous twitching of the men reacting to noises. I feel the coolness of the mist around me and the stinging sweat sitting on my brow. I taste the damp of the air around me.

At mid-afternoon we stop for a meal. The wagon grinds to a halt as the driver applies the brakes. The Royal Guard falls out and forms a loose square around the wagon. The pullers move to the wagon to retrieve the stored fire wood to heat oat mix and meat. Before long Rhă-mă is mixing and cooking the oats while Pān-thě-răs sets about building the fire for roasting meat. The other guards sit or crouch nearby while one or two stay on sentry duty. We talk and joke letting our feet rest and our legs relax. There is the creaking of wagon boards and the swish of the curtain as the Supreme Ruler exits the wagon. Jumping to the floor amidst the crackle of ice, he turns back to aid his woman who is smiling and waiting for an arm. Instead of an arm she is swept up as the Supreme Ruler lifts her slight frame in his strong arms. She giggles and he smiles as he sets her on her feet. She seems better to be on the move. She stands but continues to hold his arm as they walk to the fire. The Supreme Ruler looks at us and bids us sit as we have all snapped to attention. He sits down with his cape around his partner's shoulders and she clinging to his waist, for support. He turns to us, "Around others we will be formal, precise and scrupulous however when there is no one but us we can be flexible, frank and familiar. If you have any worries or problems with my decisions you will not question me in public, on that I must insist, you can however talk to me in private with all honesty. Now, when will the food be ready to eat?" At that point we relax and fall out of our salutes.

While the smell of roasting meat fills my nostrils, I take up my spear to check the oiling of the blade. I focus on making it perfect when a small voice beckons me from my work. I look up to face the question but I smile and apologise saying I was distracted. The Supreme Sovereign repeats her inquiry as to what I am doing. Her voice is soft but with a hint of command. She may look delicate, but she can burn with a fire if kindled. I clear my throat and she smiles at my inability to frame my words. I clear my throat again and answer her as best as I can, explaining how the blade must work free and slick. The Supreme Ruler is talking to Kē-phās about training. Rhă-mă, a slight but tall man, begins to ladle out the hot mix, passing the platter to Pān-thĕ-răs who cuts generous portions of meat before passing out the plates. I finish explaining to the Sovereign and she thanks me, taking the bowl of hot food passed to her. As the meal comes to completion we have time to rest before we make the final push of our journey, as we are making good progress.

Some of the guards sprawl on the ground and drift into light sleep, their hats pulled over their eyes.

Hy-pă-tōs, one of the inventors, rummages in the baggage looking for his belongings. With a rustle he pulls out something wrapped in a soft cloth. He unwraps a strange object, it looks like a pipe with wood worm, and it is covered in round holes. He sits down on the stone he has been warming for a while and raises the object to his mouth. The other inventor warrior, Nō-ē, sits up to ask what it is. Hy-pă-tōs smiles and puts the mouth piece to his lips. Suddenly a lovely sound like bird's singing or a woman's voice begins. He has designed a way to make music. I continue to listen as he plays, but then on top of the lovely sound is another sound. There are two lines of music, one is high but the other is lower. It sounds like a man and woman singing together. After, performing a range of tunes, Hy-pă-tōs lowers the instrument from his lips with a grin. "This is one of the secrets of my bloodline, an invention of my grandsire to pass the long nights of winter away. We have kept it safe, perfecting it and learning the finer points of it. I call it the Double Long Horn. The reason for the two horns is obvious when I start playing." He begins, but only uses his left hand. After warming up the left pipe plays a low stead note. He then uses his right hand to play a high note. He lowers the horns to explain. "By using the two pipes I can make more noises than one single pipe. The holes give the notes voices and variation." He begins to play using both pipes. After a long tune with many different tunes woven in, he puts the horn down and then wraps it back up.

The Ruler looks up to the sun marking its passage across the sky; he stands and gives the order to continue on the journey. Pān-thĕ-răs collects the plates and wipes them, then he packs them away for the journey. I stamp out the fire and scatter the ash to stop the embers reigniting. The wagon haulers take up their harnesses again and take up the strain. The companion and the Rulers go back to the wagon. With a squeal and a grate the brakes release and the wagon begins to roll forward smoothly. The haulers lean into their ropes and the guards retake their places around the wagon. The final leg of the journey is mostly uphill so some of the guard, including Kē-phās, take turns with the haulers in heaving the wagon. I would have liked to join them, but I must be the captain and keep my eyes open.

We arrive at headquarters late in the afternoon, breathing heavily from climbing the snow slide that leads up to the main gate. This narrow causeway of ice and stone never melts and becomes slippery in winter with the snowfall. Even in summer this pass is dangerous. But we negotiate the pass with little difficulty, and are welcomed home to a chorus of sentinel horns.

That evening after a large meal, we bed down on thick comfortable mats. Hy-pă-tōs once again draws out his double horn. He looks to the dying embers of the fire and with shadows leaping and twisting on his face begins a tune. It starts quietly, just a whisper above the wind swirling around the barracks. It is soft and gentle, almost a caress like a mother comforting a scared child. It grows in strength, but never becomes more than a quiet voice. It is slow and measured, calming and tranquil. The horn speaks in two voices like a mother and a child's voice. It soothes and pacifies. My heart slows and the world around me grows dim. The tune seems to ring in my ears, it runs with my blood and stills my heart to its core. Worries and troubles seem to fall from me, and still the music plays on. The world's passage grows even more dim; the music seems to block all else. I cannot resist its charm and I find myself slowly settling down on my mat, losing all control. My eyelids become heavy; they are unable to remain open. The last thing I remember is seeing Hy-pă-tōs sitting by the fire and wondering how he can remain awake, resisting his charmed pipes. His eyes glinting as he stares into the flames. The mists remain swirling around in the cool night air.

Summer in the mountains is short, and preparing for winter is a top priority. The few crops we can grow from narrow ledges need harvesting and storing. Forage needs to be cut and dried to feed our animals over the winter months when the grass will be under snows. Our herds need thinning to ensure their survival and the slaughtered animals need preserving. Our lumber must be carefully collected, dead wood and ripe trees. A week after arriving, these activities are underway and as ever we assemble in the afternoon, the Rulers and all the Royal Guards, in the Throne Room to receive the reports of the day. An official enters to read the reports from the villages and outposts. With him he brings large stone tablets, which he has received from the different bloodlines. The tablets are covered in chiselled writing from the governors of the villages. There is nothing new to report, most industry is back to full strength and all the settlements are running smoothly. Preparations for winter are going well. There is however one issue that is brought to attention. There is a blood group of the Ă-kay-dăs that has not returned yet from an extended journey to the far stores. They should have been back a day or so ago. The blood group is under the command of Stră-thōn. At this point I sit up and take notice. It is unusual for them to be late, but I am not worried. Once my sire and dam saw me to Headquarters they were re-joining the rest of the blood group to take them home. They probably stopped at places to celebrate memories, or else they have wagon trouble.

After the meeting Hy-pă-tōs approaches me, asking if he may go to his blood group to honour his sire. "Will there be more music such as you play on your horns?" I ask, a scheme seeding itself in my mind. Hy-pă-tōs nods and his brow knots as he ponders the reason behind my question. "Is it possible for there to be a guest?" I question. Hy-pă-tōs' heavy brows quickly relax and with a smirk he nods. "As long as you can remain awake this time!" he mischievously replies. "Meet me when the evening bell chimes at the barracks and I shall take you to the gathering." With that he bows and joins the flow of people leaving the hall to finish their work before night forces them to stop.

At the allotted time I meet Hy-pă-tōs in the barracks, under one arm he carries his Double Long Horns in their case, and a single horn under the other. As he sees me he nods and gestures to the door. I pick up a cloak and step out into the cool evening. Hy-pă-tōs closes the door and begins walking to where his blood group are gathering for the evening's entertainment. As we arrive we are hailed. Hy-pă-tōs bows low, betraying his dam as the woman that has come to great us. After speaking a while with him, she turns and greets me formally. "Welcome Captain, please come inside and join us in food and song." I bow to her and follow her inside. The atmosphere is warm and friendly. As last to enter, we are hailed by the rest of the company who turn to greet Hy-pă-tōs and then see the surprise visitor. Men muster and pull straight their capes and brush down their armour. Women raise their eyebrows and murmur to each other behind their hands. I ask Hy-pă-tōs to present me to his sire to pay my respects. Hy-pă-tōs' sire is very much like him, large shoulders, although smaller than mine and tall but well built. He seems overjoyed at having the Captain of the Royal Guard present at the event. After the due introduction and the custom of paying respect he begs leave of me to begin the proceeding. I smile at his formalities, "Tonight I sit as a friend of Hy-pă-tōs not as Captain. There is no need for such formality."

He moves in close to fire and calls for quiet. "Tonight, we celebrate my seeing my fiftieth winter. We have food, we have drink and we have music. Enjoy yourselves." As he finishes he nods to a tall man carrying a horn. The large man raises the horn and plays a deep mournful note followed by a higher one. Immediately the atmosphere changes, it becomes excited but hushed as the hornists assemble and warm their instruments in preparation. Hy-pă-tōs' sire has sat me next to him. As a guest, friend of Hy-pă-tōs and Captain of the Royal Guard, I have prime position next to him.

Hy-pă-tōs' sire, My-rōn, makes it his task to explain the melodies to me. There are five hornists. Three carry the long horns while the other two, one being Hy-pă-tōs himself, have Double Long Horns. They stand in a semi-circle with the tall man who called the evening to order, in the middle, facing them. He raises his hand and the hornists raise their instruments. With a nod of his head and a flourish of his hands, the musicians begin their playing. The single horns begin playing; first they blow low notes and hold them. They create a continuous sound by taking turns to breathe. Occasionally, one will run up and down his horn adding new notes and rhythms to the melody. I nudge My-rōn, "Does this tune have a name?" My-rōn laughs, "This is not a tune but their warm up exercises." As My-rōn continues to laugh, I smile and settle back into my furs to await the real music to start. Once the large horns are warmed, the smaller horns begin their exercises.

Meanwhile I am approached by Hy-pă-tōs' younger brother. He wants to talk to me about a new type of spear he has been working on. His idea is to make longer spears and clump them together to form walls. "If you can make a wall of spears thick enough, it should be impenetrable. This would act as a shield for lighter troops or defending weaker troops. You could even place warriors with large shields in the very front to make it sturdier. The only trouble is projectile weapons. We would have to field our own to counter them," He falls silent at this point upon observing my face.

"The very thought of fielding our own specialized projectile units is not one that I or many warriors would care for. Where is the honour in killing from afar and not having any scars to prove your mettle?" I continue. "It would take something drastic to make us change our minds. However this idea of a wall of spears is one that would be well received. If you could convince the wind warriors to throw their spare spears they would not find that too hard as they are still fighters and could only throw their spears a short distance. Think about it and see how it could fit your schemes."

We are interrupted by My-rōn who stands to announce the first tune of the evening. "Men and women, tonight we have a special attraction. My Heir, Hy-pă-tōs, has been given the evening off so he could play here tonight, courtesy of Āi-ās, Captain of the Royal Guard; with him shall play his younger sister, Āī-thră and others of our blood group. We shall begin tonight with a tune called Life of Man." He sits down and nods to the music leader who raises his hands and begins to countdown. The hornists raise their instruments and take breath. Then they begin their background note. Over the low hum of the horns comes the higher sound of the Long Horns. The Long Horns are played by Hy-pă-tōs and Āī-thră. They are both playing the same music, mirroring each other. It starts small and simple but then grows louder and louder, becoming more and more complicated as well as twisting. By the time the tune has finished growing there are two different tunes. By small degrees they have changed and developed, although they still bear certain resemblances. On they continue until Āī-thră breaks speed and begins to play faster. Hy-pă-tōs remains a steady speed. She however races forward, reaching a complexity that cannot be beaten. She seems to be playing at the best skill possible on this instrument. Her eyes are shut to help her concentrate, and she seems to sway as she bends this instrument to her will. She holds this while Hy-pă-tōs catches up, never becoming quicker but slowly making up the ground until he has caught Āī-thră. They then begin to weave their tunes together, firstly loosely then tighter and tighter until they are inseparable. The complexity which was incredible before is now surpassed. Individually they could inspire and be great but when combined and working together they are unforgettable. Everyone's attention is fixed to the performers, even the low rumbles of the horns are lost and forgotten. All have eyes only for Hy-pă-tōs and Āī-thră. They remain twisting their tunes with flourishes here and there as if the tunes are taking on lives of their own, growing together; threatening to separate but unwilling to be apart. They play on and on until the melody begins to age. It grows older, it loses some of its energy but in the place of energy comes delicacy and ornate. Then Āī-thră seems to fall faster, growing weaker and weaker. Hy-pă-tōs blows a few longer louder notes as if trying to encourage his sister to keep going. But she continues to fade; the horns seem to grow louder, swallowing up the tune, until it can no longer be heard. She then stops playing and lowers her horn. Hy-pă-tōs changes his tune. His tune crashes as if searching for a lost half. The tune collapses on itself like a tent that has lost its supports. He drops notes as if the melody is tumbling down.

The tune changes and becomes mournful; it wanders around as if looking for something it has lost. It deteriorates all the faster and finally the horns raise themselves one last time to swallow the tune from Hy-pă-tōs. He lowers his horn ending the tune.

After allowing the tune to fade, My-rōn stands, "There is a story behind this song and some have suggested telling it while the music plays but I feel this would rob the music of its beauty so I shall briefly tell the tale now. The horns represent the world. They play constantly as who can escape or forget the world. Hy-pă-tōs plays the tune of Man. Āī-thră plays the tune of Woman. Both begin the same way as they both are formed and grow. They then become different as boy grows into man and girl into woman. They both try to build their lives apart and finding this too hard, they decide to combine forces and ally. They build their lives together, relying on each other and all the time growing more powerful. They grow to their most powerful, crowning their achievements. But then age catches up as the horns grow in strength becoming stronger and threatening to overcome and engulf the man and woman. The struggle proves too much for one and falling into shadow, the other is left to fend alone. Weak and crack, their achievements, so strong when combined, crumble to dust and ashes when apart. The single person becomes a simple shell and eventually the world rises again and swallows all trace of both the man and the woman. A sobering thought. But now let us move to a lighter hearted piece." He raises his hands for silence then claps them in a dramatic gesture to continue the music. "Music master, begin The Warrior's Game."

There is a general chatter of anticipation and excitement following this order. The spectators move back, forming a large space in front of the musicians' seats. Two men fully suited in mountain armour take their places in the centre of the opening. The musicians move back allowing them space and after a few notes to keep their instruments warm they raise their instruments and prepare to play. The warriors, standing easy, now lower their spears and brace their shields. They instantly have my attention as I being to guess at what will happen next.

The Music Master raises his stave and with a dramatic flourish we begin.

The music strikes up a quick tempo beat. Two long horns take the melody, played by Hy-pă-tōs and his brother, the warriors begin circling around each other. They dart and twirl, thrust and recoil; all it appears in time to the music. But something does not seem right. I focus on the horns, realising they are controlling the movements of the fighters. How the horns play determine what the warriors do. I marvel at the skill and speed at which the warriors act out their instructions from the Long horns. Hy-pă-tōs plays louder and his warrior shows strength, pushing forward, while the brother plays quieter, his tune putting his warrior on the defensive. And so it continues, with the warriors circling, testing each other's defences, all the time controlled by the horns. The spectators cheer and clap as the warriors struggle on, and then it is all over Hy-pă-tōs pushes his warrior forward who knocks down the other warrior his spear tip stopping within a fingers breadth of the warrior's throat. The cheering grows and as My-rōn calls for quiet at the warriors both stand and rest easy.

"Quiet, quiet, settle down. Since that battle was over quickly I propose we start the game again." He calls to a renewed cheering. As he sits back down he nods to the music master who turns back to the musicians. The warriors lower their visors and raise their shields and spears.

After many more battles, the evening draws to a close and My-rōn thanks everyone, wishing them safe journeys. Hy-pă-tōs plucks at my sleeve and remarks that we should be leaving. I agree and we move for the exit. As we leave, people shout farewells and we answer as many as we can. As we make our way back to the Royal Compound, talking about the evening, the mist that has remained since we arrived at Headquarters begins to thin.

CHAPTER 4

As DAWN BREAKS and the sun returns I am awoken as somebody shakes my shoulder. I roll over to find Pān-thĕ-răs kneeling beside me. He is obviously distressed and I ask for a report, the grogginess of sleep quickly leaving me.

"My pardon for troubling you, Captain. The sentries have seen a large smoke column rising in the east. The Rulers are not awake yet and the gate is still barred. Should we send a scouting party to check the area?" I sit up, and pull on a thick cloak over my vest while my mind attempts to form a solution.

"It would be unwise to awake the Rulers unduly. I shall come to the stockade to see for myself. Return to the wall I will be with you shortly." Pān-thĕ-răs bows and leaves, letting the curtain fall back into place. I pull on my mail coat, pick up my helmet and take my spear from the rack as I push past the curtain, making my way to the wall.

As I leave the barracks, I see the sentries crowded together at the northern end of the compound. The day is very young with dawn still an hour or two away, judging by the glow in the east. The mist from the night before has moved off and is clustered in a few remaining pockets of cooler air. There are only a few men around at this time, mainly headquarter orderlies and sentries. There is the sound of bellows from the forge and the fires are being lit on the cooking stoves for bread. As I turn to head towards the north, I see more sentries gather at the observation tower and my stomach feels uneasy. I begin to jog now, defiantly, aware that something is not right. I climb the steps to the ramparts and past the sentries, who move aside with a bow seeing the white spear at my side. I climb the ladder to the observation platform joining Pān-thĕ-răs, Yĭ-ăn-nī and Yă-nnī. They bow as I climb up the hatch, then turn back towards the north, watching the smoke column looming up from behind a mountain. If it were not for the height of the column, the smoke would be indistinguishable from the banks of mist. The mountain itself is called Misty because of the clouds which usually encompass it; it is a five hour march from headquarters of account of the difficult passages.

I turn to the twins who look as if they have been on guard most of the night, judging from their eyes. "When was the column first sighted?" Yĭ-ăn-nī speaks up in a voice low from fatigue. "My Captain, it was first sighted when the light began to grow. We were inspecting the east stockade when I turned and saw it, I called Yă-nnī and we both came up here to investigate. Then once agreed it was smoke rather than mist, I called to Pān-thĕ-răs on the western stockade to fetch you."

It does not take me long to decide on a course of action. "Pān-thĕ-răs sound the warning horn. Yĭ-ăn-nī fetch the rest of the Royal Guard to the Throne Hall. Yă-nnī go and assemble a scouting party. Be ready by the Northern gate and draw rations for three days. I will go to the Ruler and inform him, asking him to approve the plans. With chance it will be one of the bloodlines." With a final glance over to the smoke, I turn back to the ladder and climb back down.

The sound of activity increases as I hurry to Ruler's sleeping quarters. The horn blows over the camp in a low sombre tone. The camp becomes alive with activity, men race around collecting armour and supplies, rubbing sleep from their eyes and preparing for action. As I enter the building, the door guards raise their spears, the warning horn has made them jumpy. As I approach, they recognize me and stand to attention.

I nod to them, "Be easy, there are no attacks in progress. Any sign of the Rulers?" They shake their heads. I breathe deeply to appear relaxed and easy. I raise my hand and knock on the door. There is the sound of movement inside and the Ruler voice can be heard.

"Ruler, a smoke column has been sighted to the North. I advise and request that the gates be opened to allow a small scouting party out." There is the sound of movement and the door opens and the Ruler steps out.

"We will proceed to the Throne room to better assess the situation, as we march you must inform me as to the facts." By the time we reach the throne room I have given him all the facts I know. In the board room the entire Royal Guard is assembled, standing to attention before the throne. They fall quiet and stand to attention as we enter. The Ruler sits down on the throne and I stand to his left. In front of us stand Pān-thĕ-răs, Yĭ-ăn-nī and Yă-nnī. Quickly they describe what happened until the point of my arrival. They then stop, allowing me as the senior officer to continue. Once all is finished I appeal to the Ruler for his decision. The Ruler stands and raises the black spear of command; at this sign all present fall to one knee to listen to the Ruler's instructions.

He begins, "My decision is final and is to be carried out perfectly. The Northern Gate is to be opened in a short while when the next bell tolls. A scouting group of fifty warriors will be placed under the command of Āi-ās, Captain of the Royal Guard. With him will go Pān-thĕ-răs, Yĭ-ăn-nī and Yă-nnī as guides and five War Gang Masters. They will draw rations for three days and carry full armour and weaponry. They will proceed with all speed to ascertain the source of the smoke. They will investigate the area and report back. You have your orders, you will follow them."

In the allotted time fifty good men under the command of five War Gang Masters are awoken from the barracks, armoured up, rations stored in satchels and assembled in marching order by the main gate. The gate keeper, on the sound of the Chiming Bell, removes the bar from the gate and to the groaning of the hinges, the gate rolls back to give us passage through the stockade out into the cold, misty morning. The Ruler comes out dressed in furs to watch our departure. I march up the side of the column inspecting the troops. At the head stand Pān-thĕ-răs, Yă-nnī and Yĭ-ăn-nī. I take my place with them and give the order to march. Behind me fifty left feet step smartly, as the column begins to roll forward. As we pass the Ruler our heads snap to the right, saluting to him. As we pass through the gate I give the order to march faster and we pick up the pace. The paths are unnaturally quiet; brooding and intimidating. I take comfort from the tramp, tramp of marching feet.

The journey is made in silence, as at this time in the morning the men are subdued, and unsure of what they are going to encounter. The air is cold and chilling. We make good progress, marching swiftly over the mountain passes north, maintaining a forced pace to reach the target quickly. At lunch time we stop for a quick meal. Then we forge ahead, making our way along the pass. All the time the smoke column grows bigger, but there is a new column now, rising next to it of darker smoke, as if a new fire has broken out. At mid-afternoon we reach the slopes of Misty, we only need to march around the hill and then we shall be upon the source of the smoke. Not just one smoke column, but many, although most are not big enough to be seen from Headquarters. I halt the column and give the order for open order formation. I call out for the War Gang Masters to follow me. "I shall take a look, be ready to bring the warriors up if I blow alarm on the horn. In the meantime, make camp and find some fuel for a fire. Sends some scout runners back to report we have arrived. Stay alert." With my final instructions given, my escort and I advance.

As we turn the corner, my nose reels under the assault of many odours. There is the smell of burning wood and canvas from the wagons. Above all there is the odour of spilt blood, the sourness of it making my nose tingle. There is the stench of burnt flesh. My stomach cramps and knots at the assault of the smells. My entire will is bent trying to walk on, every step to fight the urge to run away. But the smells are the least of the horrors confronting me. My eyes burn but I cannot blink or remove them from the spectacle before me. The wagons have been burnt to the ground, charred wood and smouldering canvas is all that is left of them. But I ignore them, the smell of burning flesh is more pressing on my mind. Where is it coming from? I cannot see any bodies from the front, as the wagons block my view, I walk forwards although with every step my mind tells me to run away least a deadly peril should enshroud me. But something stops me from running, whether it be a morbid fascination or being struck numb, my mind cannot give the order to flee the danger. I make my way up to the remnants of the first wagon. I see the wheel has fallen into a deep pit dug on the road and covered by loose snow, the axle has shattered. Beside the wagon I find a footprint, not a human but a creature. Such as I have never seen. It has five claws, long and pointed. The mark is big, wider than my hand. I crouch beside it, studying what it can mean. Then I understand; that the creature stood here after running over the snow kicking it about. The track is easy to follow. I trace it back across the path to find the origin of it. I walk back along the tracks finding that the creature was waiting behind a gully. This was no accident but planned, ambush.

I order my escort to hold ground then march around the wagon, preparing for the unknown. A pile of corpses are heaped around a standard and the sight chills me to the bone. Bodies I have seen, blood and gore I can stand but these bodies shake me to my most inner being and make me frightened for my life. They are mutilated and torn, most are barely recognisable as man and woman, let alone who they once were. They have been cut and dishonoured in death. Many are missing limbs and have their innards spewed in front of them, as if someone has delighted to cause pain and suffering. Most are lying in their own blood, which looks as though something has for want of a better word danced through it, as if they have delighted in death and gore. I tear my eyes from them unable to look them in their horrid slashed faces. I look at the standard that has been planted in the mass of them and I shudder pulling my cape around me at the sudden gust of chilly wind that blows around me. It is a pointed rod onto which is stuck a human head. The face is contorted beyond recognition in a chilling mask of pain and suffering; surely this person died in agony and mortal dread. The face will haunt me for the rest of my life. I drag my gaze away to look at the ground. I turn back, pale as snow and steady myself against the wagon wheel. I see the Masters looking at me inquiringly. I cannot speak, I open my mouth, but nothing comes out. I turn to call the others but I cannot. Waves of sickness flood up from my stomach and I have to use all my strength to force them back down. I lean against the charred wheel, drained of strength. They look at me confused. I put my hand over my mouth, I point back over my shoulder. The Masters walk around the wagon and I hear the sound of retching. One returns shaking his head in disbelief, paler than white stone. I tell him to go and fetch Pān-thĕ-răs. He nods and with unsteady steps walks back around the ridge. I breathe deeply to slow my frantic heartbeat.

A though crosses my mind what if the offenders are still here. I shout back over my shoulder, worry preying on my mind, "Pān-thĕ-răs, everyone back into full armour and send more warriors after the scouts." I turn back and to my now growing horror I see a new smoke column, someone has started a fire. Pān-thĕ-răs has walked around the ridge, summoned by the tone of my voice. I start running towards him shouting desperately, "Douse those flames. Kill that fire. The convoy was ambushed, we are not alone out here. Return to the warriors and send a fast runner back to Headquarters. Inform the Supreme Ruler that one convoy was ambushed. As of yet the identity of the offenders is unclear. Do it now." He spins around and gives sharp orders. Men are thrown into action and suddenly the camp is a rush of activity. Four warriors start running back to headquarters. I turn back to the wagon, steeling myself to look at the sights that will be forever seared into my mind.

I see a human hand reached out from under the pile of bodies. A woman's hand but with fingers cut off after death, the fingers that bear jewellery. And suddenly I recognize the hand. The full horror hits me; I know which convoy this is. My voice dies in my throat, my heart stops and I fail to my knees chocking on my sobs. Pān-thĕ-răs looks at me in concern, as I reach forward and stroke the outstretched hand; the hand that nurtured me and cared for me in sickness and comforted me in fear. The hand that above all I want to feel comfort from now. My dam's hand. This is my close bloodline's convoy and these mutilated and torn bodies the remains of my family. My world is shattering into thousands of little shards, each ripping and tearing at me, causing me more pain than any cut. They are all dead. I desperately push at the mound, heaving the corpses aside, blood splattering on my clothes and face, trying to free my dam. I roll her over and break into wailing. She has been disfigured and mutilated; she is a mass of cuts and a mask of pain. I wail, cradling her on my knee. Pān-thĕ-răs now understands, bellows for the warriors to move themselves and then helps me. He throws himself into the corpses trying to separate them out, gasping at the wreckage of some, all the time shouting for help.

He suddenly stops and with a white face turns to me with tears in his eyes. "Āi-ās, I am so sorry, but I think have found your sire." He struggles to say, in voice that is choked with grief. I look into his eyes and I see pity and pain. I cover my dam with my cloak, steeling myself to see my sire. I break into new wailing. The tears rolling freely down my cheek, I sob, moan and wail. My world is crashing down in front of my eyes and I cannot stop it. I cannot describe the pain for there he lies still with his brown fur cloak on. His once strong body is broken and torn, his fingers gone, his fine clothes torn and bloodied, but worst of all his chest, a mass of broken bones and mangled flesh. His head is gone and his neck is torn and cut. The pain is too much for me to take, I crash to my knees weeping like a child in the midst of nightmares but from this one there is no waking. There can be no loving sire to wake me or dam to reassure me, for they both lie before me dead and unrecognizable. I desperately look around trying to find his head and then my eye falls on the standard. My hand covers my mouth, trying to stifle my wails, as I struggle through the corpses to it. The head, unrecognizable and horrific, becomes my worst nightmare. The hair once dark and long is now dripping with blood and covered in mud. It is my sire. The last of my will dies and I fall to the ground in a fever.

I open my eyes to feel the cold of snow settling on me, I cannot see, darkness has fallen. That is not the only darkness and the events of before come flooding back to me. I sit bolt upright, remembering the bodies of my loved ones, shouting, being angry and heart dead all at once. In my raving, I feel hands grasp me, trying to hold me down. I throw them off like a mad man and struggle to my feet. I am babbling, calling for my dam and my sire, begging them to come back to me. Someone throws himself at my legs and I tumble back onto the ground. I knock my head and it seems to awaken me. The madness leaves me, leaving only a dead heart and fear. I feel someone grab me and in my fear I think it the creature that killed my sire and dam. I struggle to throw him off shouting for help. He talks to me, trying to calm me. I grab his cloak and pull him forward into the light of the fire. It reveals a very worried and concerned Kē-phās, but my mind must be playing tricks how can Kē-phās be here? I shout all the louder, my fears threatening to break into madness once again. Kē-phās tries his best to hold me down, but I throw him off. I rise again and run, being chased by cries and footfalls. I run back around the ridge and hurry back to my loved ones. I stop dead, the sound of feet stopping behind me. My knees start wobbling and begin to buckle; I feel strong arms under me as I sag to the ground like an old man losing his life breath. Before me is laid my blood group in their death veils. They are tended, some dignity restored to them. I pull back the veil of my dam and my sire weeping to see that this is no dream or sickness-driven madness. I sit and stare, unable to understand the ruins of what was once my world.

The warriors have finished making my blood group decent; it is then that I remember my sibling. I run to the other bodies searching desperately dreading what has happened to him, but I cannot find him and other members of my bloodline are missing. A spark of hope flares in my heart, maybe he is still breathing. My heart soars but my head brings it back to earth with the thought: Where is he? I fear the worst and I crumble into new tears at the thought of losing him too. Exhausted, I stand and meekly allow myself to be led away, but then I pick up my bed and struggle back to my blood group. I will spend my final night with them, surrounded by my loved ones. The ground is cold and icy pressed against my skin but it cannot match the coldness of my heart. I have lost my strength and warmth, the world has not much left for me now. My heart feels empty and dead.

The next days are most painful for me. It feels as if our whole nation has turned out for the mourning of our loss. Indeed so many people have been lost that almost everyone has been affected by this event. They are entombed in the bloodline cave. I stand at the top of the world, as Captain of the Royal Guard, second only to the Ruler, but I stand alone. The failure of my blood line now rests with me.

The night after the funeral march, I am in the Headquarter Barracks. I sit staring into the fire thinking and brooding. I cannot throw the image of the standard and destruction out of my head. Every time I lay my head down to rest, the scenes flash before me and I awake covered in sweat. Who can have done this and what is capable of such aggression, to attack a convoy with women, children and few warriors? How could someone be so dishonourable? A knock on the door pulls me from my broodings, I stand to open the door and allow my visitor in. To my relief I see Nīk-ă-tōr; it is heart-warming to see him alive before me. His face is pale and hard. His eyes are bloodshot and tired.

He gives me a watery smile and embraces me. "Āi-ās, I am sorry for not being at the funeral but I have only just heard. I was away on a scouting mission for the Ruler and have just returned. Let me make this clear that if you should need anything, you only have to ask. My blood group will be happy to help in any way possible. Stră-thōn was a great warrior and I would honour his offspring as if they were my own." I thank him and ask him to sit. We spend time talking. I have not spoken to anyone of what I have seen, finding it too hard. But to an old friend of my sire it is easy to unburden my mind. He talks with me, revealing his deepest thoughts to me and worst nightmares. He finishes and sits back to allow me time to make sense of all that has been said. My mind races, it twists and turns trying to understand the full implications. I try to speak but the words will not form.

He nods at my inability to frame words, "When I had finished trying to think this through, I also had that exact trouble. But come the night is too dark to think upon that, let us speak of another matter, although this could prove as hard to understand. I am not young, indeed I may not see many more winters. As you know my bloodline will end with me. When my blood group left me, Ē-vĭŏs, my dear Heir having the accident and his dam, my poor Ky-rǎ, dying of grief, it was the end of my line. All that was left to me was Kǎ-llī-ōpē." He speaks, not to me, but as if trying to preserve the memory.

He grimaces, "It had been our plan to give her to Ē-vĭŏs. How wrong we were to tempt the elders. I was friend to her father and as he died he committed her care to me. Before my life breath leaves me I must give her care to another. How old are you? Eighteen? It is time for you to find your life ally. You like her, I know and I do not think your attention will be unwelcome. This is not official, but is a friendly word."

I blink and bow to him. "My grief and sorrow will not let me yet, so I will wait. But I have heard." I reply.

He shakes his head, "Her family was killed when she was young, so she knows what it is like to lose a world. She also knows what it is like to build a new life. She is perfect for you. To move on you must rebuild before you are sealed in your gloom."

"But how can I forget them?" I ask angrily.

"Have I said as much?" he says sharply, "You will never forget but you can still live." He says softly. With these parting words he stands and leaves.

The morning finds me walking the stockade. The visit of Nīk-ǎ-tōr has brought me much to think on. My heart still feels frozen, numbed by the past days, but my will has reasserted itself and I can work again, although the scars on my heart will endure for all time. I have emptied my heart of all weakness and now only hatred and rage remain, and a determination to find the killers. A horn sounds, calling the Royal Guard to the throne room. I turn quickly and march rapidly to the hall. I find most of the guards assembled and the rulers seated in their chairs, their faces grim and strained. Once the last guards arrive the doors are shut and barred to prevent disruption.

The Ruler stands to address us, "Not long ago runners arrived from every village. It seems we are under attack from the south. I am declaring a national emergency. The bulk of our flocks lie dead, slaughtered during the night, with the herders dead. The crops have been burnt to cinders, only what is stored in the granaries remains. Lastly, our furthest outposts have fallen silent: Although this could be a communication problem, we fear these outposts have fallen." At this point he stands and raises the Black Spear of command.

We all kneel as the Supreme Ruler issues his orders. "Guards, we are under attack and we need to act. We cannot go up further into the hills, crops cannot grow and our flocks will die. We must descend the slopes and return to the plains. I want groups of scouts out and looking for a way down. The groups will leave today. They will report back within fourteen days."

By mid-day the scouting groups are ready to leave. Iă-rĕt and Nă-ŏs command one group that will be going directly South from headquarters. Pān-thĕ-răs and Nĭk-ōm-ēdēs will lead another group west until they reach the Kōr-ăx village, then head South-West. Finally Bĭ-ōn and Hy-mēn will travel east until they hit the Scy-thĕs village and then they will turn South-East. They each have a group of fifty men, a mix of Wind and Mountain warriors. Their orders are to search for seven days. If they find a route through, they are to return and send runners ahead. After seven days or if they encounter any significant military presence, they are to return to headquarters with all speed. After the tramp of boots has died down, I go to find Ruler Krē-ōn. I have been thinking, what I conclude chills me and I wish to confer with him. I find him seated in the throne room deep in thought. I clear my throat and wait for him to acknowledge me.

He stirs himself and looks to me with a watery smile on his face. "It seems that while we have been playing games, our enemies have been watching and waiting. The full story is much worse. At each attack a standard was left. One of the heads was lopped off and stuck on a post. A cross bar was attached under the skull and from it were hung teeth; not human but animal, daggers sharp. I feel your loss; Stră-thōn's wise counsel is missed in these dark times. Do you bring any thoughts with you?" I bow and walk over to the campaign map. I stand there, waiting for the Ruler to join me.

He looks at me and then stands and walks over to the other side of the map facing me. "Supreme Ruler, I petition you to commission another scouting group. I volunteer to lead this group and I would ask for it to travel North into the very heart of the mountains. If our other scouts fail to find a way through, we can at least retreat back into the mountains if we are overrun. We do not yet know what attacked us, although the scouts might find them sooner than they expected." The Ruler looks from me to the map and back to me again.

He considers my argument. "How far north would you travel?"

"I would go further than we have ever been before. We must know the land and what is there so that we can retreat should we need to. We have learnt something about our foes; They are bloodthirsty and cruel. We must be ready, if need be to move. It might be too late to leave by the time the other groups return. We may have stirred our foes to action by then."

The Ruler looks at me and with a deep sigh studies the map. His eyes skim over the planned routes of the other forces then veer away to the north of the map until they reach the edge; the furthest point of our knowledge.

I continue, "There is however one further argument I must add. I suspect we have an issue of loyalty. All our routes through the mountains are hidden and secret. The convoy was ambushed. I saw clearly they had waited for the right moment; there were footprints where they had waited then charged out. My question is how they managed to find the route without being seen. No outposts were attacked and none reported troop movement in the area. Somebody turned a blind eye. We must sound out the Battle Masters and deal with traitors. I must also ask that my scouting group is not mentioned in public, nor given an official send off. We must move quickly to prevent talk."

"Take Kē-phās and Nīk-ă-tōr along with two other Royal Guards. I would recommend that you take the Ninth Mixed Ă-kay-dăs War Band. They are up to full strength; Thirty mountain warriors and twenty wind warriors. They are well officered and are a veteran unit. They are also recruited from your home settlement; you might know them and will understand them. You will leave tomorrow at midnight. You will take two wagons with you to carry extra weapons, fuel and rations. You must be back within four moon cycles to report. Until then, I want you to send runners back if major events occur. As you go, map the area looking for; natural resources, land features and other useful information. Leave now and make all preparations." I bow and leave, pulling the doors shut behind me and leaving the Supreme Ruler to his thoughts.

That evening Nīk-ă-tōr arrives as agreed and with the other Royal Guards I have chosen, we sit down to a meal to discuss our plan of attack. Along with me and Nīk-ă-tōr are Kē-phās, Yă-nnī and Yĭ-ăn-nī along with a senior mapper Dry-ăs. I open the discussion with the objectives of the expedition.

"We are currently being faced with the biggest threat to our security in a generation. It is doubtful to me that the other scout groups will be successful. Instead of going down the slopes, we need to find refuge in the mountains."

At this point Yă-nnī interrupts me. "How can we move up? Our crops cannot grow and our flocks will die of starvation because the soil is too thin. What hope is there in the mountains except death and dishonour?"

I nod. "This is the reason I have invited Nīk-ă-tōr. He was one of the scout groups that first went up into the mountains, as far as the Wailing Pass. As you are aware, Nīk-ă-tōr was the Royal Mapper under the last Ruler, so he will be in charge of making the maps. Dry-ăs is to help him and provide a secondary mapper. Our main aim is to find information and expand our knowledge north. We are looking for items and resources that could make it habitable for us, if we are forced to retreat. Our escort will consist of thirty Mountain warriors and twenty Wind warriors, the Ninth Mixed Ă-kay-dăs. Our inventory must be only essential items such as fuel, food, weaponry and scouting equipment. We will travel to edge of our knowledge and keep going. Within four moon cycles we must be back to report. I have put my plans to the Ruler and with his full backing I have been granted supplies and man power. The full convoy will contain the following; the Ninth Mixed Ă-kay-dăs, two wagon masters, sixteen haulers, two wagons with supplies and us. We shall be ready to leave tomorrow at midnight." As I end the briefing I sit back to allow questions to be asked.

Dry-ăs, who has been eating, puts his plate down and sits forward indicating his query. "Do we have any information on threats in the area or will we be working blind?" he aims the question towards Nīk-ă-tōr. Nīk-ă-tōr finishes his mouthful and takes up the reply. "I can only talk about the situation nine winters ago when the last expedition was sent. I was head of the group and its purpose was to identify the possibility of oat ground. The land was deemed to be unusable. During the expedition itself there were no military threats either from the environment or enemies; the main danger was the weather. The temperature falls the further you travel north. We must be equipped with furs and plenty of fuel. We shall be taking plenty of extra clothes and food, as well as winter tents. However we were not under attack back then, so I advise that now we should treat the land as hostile and full of unknown dangers."

I sit forward again to impart the most important part of the brief. "What I am about say is left within these walls. It is not mentioned to anyone else apart from those gathered here and it is not mentioned without me or Nīk-ă-tōr present in the conversation. Failure to comply with this will mean exile or possible execution for treason. We have possible traitors working against us. Our departure is not to be mentioned or talked about. As far as those outside are concerned we are carrying on as normal. No one will see our departure. This is not a request but an order from the Ruler himself, so we must comply exactly, without question." All had stopped eating and focused on me. Nīk-ă-tōr is watching me and glancing to the others. It was his scheme as originally proposed and he is well placed to watch reactions. Yă-nnī and Yĭ-ăn-nī are watching me, not showing emotion or giving anything else away. Dry-ăs looks pale, his face contorted into a frown, trying to understand the implications of this brief. Kē-phās is just eating, no worrying about details just will he have enough to fill his stomach on this trip.

Nīk-ă-tōr takes up the thread, "At midnight the watch will change. The north gate is being told to take up their guard late. The gap between watches is when we begin our journey. Warriors and the convoy will not be assigned or informed until the evening to prevent leaks. They will then be confined to barracks until the convoy is ready to leave." Once this part of the brief is complete we settle to eat and discuss finer details. We are solemn and sober with the details of this expedition. The evening finishes with us retiring to the sleeping quarters.

The next day dawns the same as any other. I wake early and sit by the fire, my mind drifting back to the events of the ambush. I frown, struggling to banish the thoughts from my head, but they roar and laugh at my attempts to block the mutilated bodies and carnage or the wagons. I feel a hand on my shoulder. In my tortured state I jump and spin around, screaming my rage. I find Kē-phās frowning at me, looking worried.

I lapse back, allowing Kē-phās to sit next to me. "You were having night terrors." I sigh and slump forward.

Kē-phās looks at the fire, "When I was seven my sibling was crushed by a runaway wagon. Our bloodline has been convoy workers for most of their time. The slope was icy and the brakes were stiff. The haulers lost their grip and the wagon slid back. My sibling was only five, playing on the slope. I saw the danger but my voice fled, struck numb by fear. By the time I screamed the warning, the wagon was too close. He was killed outright, the wheel rolled over his chest as he tried to roll out of the way. I can still remember his face as he turned to see the wagon sliding towards him. I have blamed myself for the weakness ever since that first night." I look to Kē-phās and for the first time I see his true face. I see it pained and troubled.

"Just one question, will I ever be free from the torments?" I ask although I know the dreaded answer. Kē-phās looks to me with sadness in his eye and shakes his head slowly. I break down and cradle my head in my hands. Kē-phās puts an arm over my shoulder and embraces me as a sibling; he is the one person that understands my plight and pain.

CHAPTER 5

Night falls slowly, it creeps across the sky eating light and shrouding all in mystery. The settlements grind to a halt for the night, but as one task is finished another begins to function. The warriors are briefed and confined to their barracks. The convoy is alerted and the wagon masters, a man and his woman, send their labourers scurrying around making things ready. Food is preserved and crated; stacked weapons are oiled and bundled; ropes are coiled and bound; fuel is cleaned and dried. The wagons are loaded and secured, the axles oiled to make them soundless and the wheels are scrutinized for defects. The nineteenth bell sounds, one chime before the changing of the sentries. Under cover of darkness, Nīk-ă-tōr, Yă-nnī, Yĭ-ăn-nī, and I steal across the settlement, meeting the warriors at the barracks and taking them to the wagon compound. We assemble in marching formation and prepare to move out. I am busy making final checks, moving down the line of warriors making sure they are ready. I see some familiar faces that were with me on the last expedition. Most of the warriors are heavily wrapped in furs to protect them from the cold, but one seems more wrapped than the others, he also stands slightly apart as if he is not familiar with the rest of the warriors. He wears a cloak with a deep hood obscuring his face and with a scarf wrapped over it meaning all that I can see is the eyes and the top of his nose. I turn to continue making checks. I think nothing more of the observation. Moving back up to the head of the column. I see an old veteran clinging to a long leather tube instead of a spear; one of our most precious possessions. Inside safe from wind and weather, wrapped in thick furs is The Ruler's Standard. The Standard was presented to this group of warriors when they were formed as recognition for their service to the bloodlines. Only now the aged warrior is joined by another warrior who carries the Royal Guard's Colours. A new sound pulls away my attention. A horn sound in the dark signalling the changing of the guard; it's time to move.

The Battle Master hisses an order and without noise or fuss the warriors fall out and form up into a marching column. The wind warriors move to the space between the wagons while the mountain warriors split into two groups; one moves to the head of the column, while the other moves to the rear. Scattered amongst the groups are torch bearers their fires hissing gently in the cool air. The Battle Master nods in satisfaction and turns back to me, awaiting my next instruction. Without a word I and the royal guards take our place at the head of the column. I throw my arm straight up into the air and behind me fifty pairs of feet come to attention and then fall silent. We are ready to move. I breathe deeply and throw my arm forward, fist closed, giving the order to move forward.

The convoy begins to march, with barely a groan the wagon begins to move forward. The soft crunch of snow and ice marks the column's movement. I hear coughing and furiously look back. The Battle Master also turns back and I see him gesturing to the unfortunate warrior. As we approach the gate, a figure steps out of the shadows, veiled in furs. As we draw level he stands tall and I dip my head in respect to the Supreme Ruler. Behind me the heads of the Ninth Mixed Ă-kay-dăs snap to the left and salute as they pass Krē-ōn. He raises an arm and clicks his fingers. Two sentries move out of the shadows, unbolt the gates and open the way for our departure. A second figure, wrapped in furs appears out of the shadow next to the Ruler. I nod and allow my face to show a smile. She moves nearer to the Ruler, they both smile and then the formality reasserts itself. Amidst the muffled jangle of armour, the slight groan of axles and heavy breathing of the wagon haulers, we leave the stockade and begin our journey into the unknown. As we march into the gloom, the early morning mists swallowing the fort up, we hear the sentries climb to the stockade to take over from the night watch.

As the sun climbs into the sky, we near the mountain passage that will take us to the very edge of our maps. Headquarters is four leagues behind us. Apart from the quiet noise of the convoy the passage is silent, the mountain ridges on either side bare of life. The only sound is the whistling of the wind. The convoy is marching quickly, all the warriors are wary, as if they are being watched. Every sound makes them tense; but can I blame them? Not so long ago I would have walked these passages fully confident, but now? The truth is that we are no longer sure. We do not know what is out there and we can only guess at what is savaging our nation. But this is no time for such questions; I must now focus on the task at hand. I look behind me, scanning the ridges for any sign of life. Breathing a sigh of relief as I cannot see anything. I look back along the convoy making sure the pace is correct. There are no stragglers, although some gaps are starting to form. I frown at the Battle Master who sees my glance and hurries back to straighten the lines. I shake my head and turn back to the route ahead. All is silent and quiet as we travel.

We make good time, marching rapidly to the edge of our lands. By evening, we have reached the very edge of our maps at the Mount of Snow so named because of its permanent crown of snow. As the light fades we set up the tents and prepare to spend our final night in our lands. The tents are rigged, the wagons parked and the labourers rest. To light fires before we leave would be to advertise our presence, so we must eat our food cold. We must make sure our secrecy is preserved. As is our custom, the tents are assembled in a circle, even though the normal fire in the centre is unlit. Just before I go to bed for the night, I walk around checking the camp. As I pass them, each of the guards outside the tent entrances salute and nod. With a final look around I bow to the other guards and approach my tent. The tent is cool but not yet unpleasantly cold. Without the fire the temperature will drop quickly. Each tent is split into two. The front is where the guards will stay when the temperature drops dangerously low, the back section is the main sleeping area. I nod to the guard, who stands to attention. It is the smaller guard that was wrapped in all the furs. He is still wrapped in the furs. I stop and look at him. He stays at attention looking straight ahead. The eyes are all I can see and they look forward without blinking. They are pale blue and they look familiar, but I cannot place them. I shrug it off and turn to the main section. As I enter the main section, I am greeted by Kē-phās, Nīk-ă-tōr and the other Royal Guards. I catch the eye of Nīk-ă-tōr and roll my eye. The twins and Kē-phās are debating the merits of Wind and Mountain warriors. It is a debate that has never been concluded and will continue all the days of our nation. I leave them to it. I sit with my back supported by one of the tent poles. I let my mind drift and slowly, surely sleep hangs heavy on my eyes. The wind howling around the tent grows quieter as I gently fall into sleep. I can still hear the debate, but it is muffled and sounds far away.

I am awoken by a hand shaking my shoulder I move to shout but a hand clamps over my mouth. My eyes flick open and I see Nīk-ă-tōr looking at me, finger on mouth. I nod and slowly he pulls his hand. I must have been asleep some time, the others are asleep and the wind has died down. I look at Nīk-ă-tōr who has moved to Kē-phās and wakes him up.

I slowly crawl over to them and put my mouth to Nīk-ă-tōr's ear, mindful of silent warning. "What watch is it? Why have you woken us up?" I ask quietly. He shrugs his shoulders and cups his ear. He wants to listen for something. Suddenly there is a sound from the back of the tent. Nīk-ă-tōr looks at me and Kē-phās and points to the direction of the sound. He begins to silently move in that direction and beckons us to follow. Full of mystery and intrigue we crawl after him but not after we have pulled our weapons close. The back of the tent, the part furthest from the fire is used to stock goods and now Nīk-ă-tōr is quietly moving the equipment away from the back so that he can access the very back, next to the heavy felt. He starts handing equipment back and we stack it out of the way. All the time Nīk-ă-tōr tries to keep as silent as possible, trying not to disturb the other sleepers. Then we hear the sound again and Nīk-ă-tōr freezes. It is as if someone is just on the other side of the tent. There is a large gap by the felt of the tent and we are all pressed near it trying to listen for more sounds. Suddenly there is the sound of snow being trodden down and something approaches right up to the other side of the tent. I can hear steady deep breathing. I tap Kē-phās on the shoulder and gesture to the sleepers. Obediently he turns to wake them up. As he crawls away I take my spear and tap him on the back. He turns to look at me and I cover my mouth with my hand and then point to the sleepers. He nods and crawls away to Yă-nnī, the closest. I turn back to continue listening to the noise outside. I bring my spear forward in case we are about to be attacked. The breathing turns broken and irregular. Nīk-ă-tōr leans over and taps my shoulder. He then mimics digging. Whatever is outside is trying to enter. I look back to where the rest of the guards are now awake. I gesture them to pick up their spears silently and then join me. I wait until all are gathered and then I gesture for them to be ready. Nīk-ă-tōr plucks at my trousers and I turn back. The curtain felt is moving as whatever is outside makes contact with it. It will not be long now. We all hold our breath as the intruder makes contact. I raise my spear ready to defend. The felt moves more as the intruder pushes against it. I turn my spear and with a grunt bring it down on the moving felt. The air is split by a squealing noise and suddenly the whole camp is alive with shouting and activity. I bellow and with the rest of the tent run through the porch, passing the guards, freezing them with shock, and plunge into the night. The moon is full and there are no clouds so there is enough light for me to see. I race around the side of the tent, bellowing my war cry. I keep my spear point down ready to throw myself at the intruder. Yĭ-ăn-nī is on my left and Yă-nnī on my right. We arrive around the back, but whatever was there has left. As the rest of the guards arrive I order everyone to stand still. There are the sounds of a something large pounding over the snow, running fast away from the camp. I shout for fire to be brought and soon the crackling of wood is heard and the torches are brought round.

"Scan the ground for tracks. I want to know who it was and which way they went." I shout at the warriors. Almost straightaway a warrior finds something and with a nerve in his voice proclaims that this was no man. I jog over to him and stare at the ground, unsure of what I see. There are footprints, but not of a man, woman or child. They are large, much bigger than my foot. They are deep; whatever made them was big and heavy. They are split along the middle, meaning the creature has two toes. This is not the same print that I found near the ambushed convoy. I crouch down in the now thick snow to study the prints better. There is a line of prints heading away from the camp.

"Yĭ-ăn-nī and Yă-nnī take a squad of warriors and follow the track for only six hundred paces. There may be more of them out there. Move out only when you are all armoured up. Take no chances." I turn to look at Nīk-ă-tōr, "Double the guards and put the camp on a war footing. Secrecy is unnecessary. Light the main fire and post torches at the edges of the camps. Perhaps fire will keep these creatures back." As the twins jog away, I hear the shouts of the Battle Master as he turns the guards out and begins to assert some order over the chaos. I start shivering, suddenly aware of the bone chilling cold of the snowflakes falling around me. The heavily furred guard suddenly appears with cloaks and hands them to me and Nīk-ă-tōr. He bows and smiles and then turns back to the trail. I take the cloak and look up to the face of the guard, those pale blue eyes again watching me, unblinking and powerful. I dip my head and turn back to the tracks.

Kneeling in the snow, I follow the tracks that approach the tent. The creature had pushed through the snow that has built up near the tent and was right up to the felt. The gap is large much wider than the length of my arm. In a matter of moments it could have been through and causing carnage. I stand up and shiver, not from the cold but dreading to think what would have happened. In the distance I can hear shouts as Yă-nnī and Yĭ-ăn-nī battle through the now thickening snow. I spin on my heels and with the guards hurrying behind me move back into the circle of tents. The camp is now awash with movement and light as the central fire is lit and stoked. All the men are up and about. No one will be able to sleep now the camp is on a war footing. Two of the guards are armed with torches that have been set alight and are placing them around the camp, creating a ring of fire. I nod, approving the precautions and duck back into my tent to talk to Nīk-ă-tōr. I send one of the guards to find him and then sit in the porch waiting for him to arrive. Behind me stands the guard who brought my cloak, the one with the pale eyes and thick furs. As I sit, I warm my arms by the fire. My arms lose their pale blue hue and slowly recover their normal colour. My blood begins to flow and I feel the heat of it sear across my skin.

Before long the tent flaps swings back and Nīk-ă-tōr enters, snow falling off his cloak. I rise to greet him and gesture for him to sit the other side of the fire.

"What are the latest reports and activity?" I query. Nīk-ă-tōr takes a breath, focusing his mind and ordering his thoughts.

"All the guards are aroused. Extra sentries have been placed both on the inside of the camp and on the outskirts. They all are carrying torches and are all accounted for. The main fire is burning brightly and I have organized the cart haulers, in shifts, to tend and protect it. The group under Yĭ-ăn-nī are still following the tracks, I have posted two guards to watch for their return." I nod, assured in the knowledge that all is under control in the camp and there will be no more surprises that night. I sit back, stretching my stiff back, then sitting forward, I allow my face to assume the Empty Face. Nīk-ă-tōr looks at me and his forehead wrinkles into a frown as he observes the change in my attitude.

"Is something troubling you?" he asks. I reply. "Two points. First, we are still in familiar territory and the nearest outpost is but ten leagues from us. That is only five leagues outside regular patrol area and yet we have never encountered this creature before. It is a conundrum that my mind is finding a challenge to pick apart. There is, however, another matter that I would ask you to consider." I breathe deeply and without hesitation pose my question.

"Why is there a woman among the guard, posing as a man?" As the question unfolds Nīk-ă-tōr, who has been deep in his thoughts, looks at me sharply.

"What is this madness that you ask of me? Which warrior do you suspect of masquerading as a man? What leads you to ask this question?" He seems bewildered; however his face does not match his voice.

"There is a woman disguised as one of the guards, for what reason I cannot at present conceive, but that fact remains we have a guard who is not what they claim." Nīk-ă-tōr blinks and seems to glance around him mainly behind me towards the guard at my back, which confirms my suspicions.

"I believe that you are aware of whom I speak." I spin backwards, knocking the guard over, pulling my dagger from its case and pressing it quickly to his neck. It is over in the blink of an eye and the guard taken by surprise struggles to free himself. However he quietens down and remains still at the look in my eye and the cold metal of my blade.

"I would remain very still if I were in your place. One false move and this would be uncomfortable."

However, I mean no threat by these words. I know exactly who is under the disguise, although I have yet to comprehend the reason for her presence. I look towards Nīk-ă-tōr, who is trying his best not to look alarmed at my drastic course of action. He has turned fairly pale and I know why he would be worried. I turn back to my captive who is watching me with those pale eyes. I pull the scarf from the guard. Out of the hood spills silver hair and the mask falls away to reveal, Kă-llī-ōpē, the adopted Heiress to Nīk-ă-tōr. I break into a smile and with care I release her, sliding my dagger back into my cloak. With a sigh, Kă-llī-ōpē wriggles around to sits next to me. She is so close I can feel the warmth from her skin. Nīk-ă-tōr breathes a deep sigh and mops his brow with his sleeve, relieved that Kă-llī-ōpē has come to no harm and happy that I am not angry.

Kă-llī-ōpē ties back her hair allowing her to watch both me and Nīk-ă-tōr.

I clear my throat "I have sent word to the Wagon masters; you shall stay in their tent since they have a women over there. The only question I have for you is, why?"

She turns to look at me with a quizzical look in her eye. "Nīk-ă-tōr is the only sire I have known, how could I be apart from him? I swore to Ky-ră that I would watch over him."

And with that she stands, bows to Nīk-ă-tōr and after pulling her deep hood over her face leaves the tent. "Now that is a woman I would not like to cross." I remark as the tent flap falls back into place sealing the cold air back outside.

CHAPTER 6

Dawn arrives in splendour. The sun slowly rises from behind the peaks in the west. It bathes the landscape in a golden hue like polished metal. But for us, we have no time to admire it. There is an almost tangible relief as the light chases the horrors and shadows of the night. It is now easy to study the ground and confirm the events of the night. The creature, large and heavy judging by the prints and pushed aside snow, worked its way up to the tent and ruffled through the snow that had built up overnight. It then ran away, presumably in surprise and hopefully in fear when I struck. The groups under Yă-nnī and Yĭ-ăn-nī have more to add to the picture. They followed the tracks of the creature, which was strong enough to run through deep snow. Once they reached the allotted distance, they stayed and listened for a while and just before they turned to leave there was the sound in the distance of a moving animal and the snow being turned aside as the creature drove deeper into blackness. They returned at this point. Yĭ-ăn-nī paused in his recollection as if deciding upon an issue. I looked towards him and indeed his face was perplexed.

He frowned and begins in a cautious voice, "As we returned I sent Yă-nnī to the front to lead the men while I followed at the back. As we travelled, I could not be certain but I felt that were we being followed. By whom or what I cannot tell, but I am certain that something was watching us. At times I looked behind and saw a shadow move but I dismissed it as tiredness and trickery. However now I am more convinced of what I saw. We were nearing the camp and presumably the fire and activity caused the shadow to stop and think twice." I sit back to consider the information. From the short time I have known Yĭ-ăn-nī; I have assessed him to be a man of true judgement. He would not bring something before me if he was not sure. If he saw something then this is good enough to be included in our planning.

I sit forward to issue instructions for the day. "Hear me and heed my words. We must continue with our task, so we shall go in to the unknown lands. We shall move as soon as we are packed." Everyone bows and then leaves the tent. All seems quiet, but only for a moment. The Battle Master begins to shout orders and the camp becomes alive with activity. Within a short period of time the tents are dropped, the fires stamped out, the wagons loaded, everyone equipped and ready to move.

The solders are called to form up in full armour. I stroll down the lines with the other Guards following behind. I do not check equipment, knowing full well that any problem will already have been jumped on by the Battle Master, I look at their faces. I see anxiety, fear and wariness but I also see courage, energy and determination. The wagons are poised ready to move. The ropes are taunt and ready for action. I see Kă-llī-ōpē perched on the wagon next to the driver and half bow in her direction. She smiles and looks away. I walk back to the head of the company and take my place behind the two forward Mountain warriors who are armed with long staffs to pummel the deep snow.

I nod to the Battle Master, standing next to me, who waits then takes a deep breath. "Muster...stand straight." There is the sound of armour clanking, as men snap to attention. Indeed the laws of parade are so strong and the training so ingrained that even I have the urge to join suit.

"Muster...prepare to march. Muster...march half pace." With the groaning of wagon wheels and the grunts of the haulers, the convoy rolls forward. With infinite care and attention to precision the warriors march together. The Battle Master, the only person allowed to break step while marching, looks around him and with a contented cluck settles into the pace.

I lean over to him and comment "Muster, increase speed". He smiles understanding my impatience. He looks back over his shoulder and gives the order. The company checks, then begins to march faster. Before long we reach the Wailing Pass. Out of the mist loom the mountains that mark the boundary of our lands. The only place to cross them is a narrow, winding passage. The wind races through the pass, piling up the snow and making it hard to navigate. The wall is the lowest part of the mountain range but it is a challenge to cross. We stop and have food at the bottom of the mountain. The meal is hot and warms us to our innermost cores. After the meal, I call the men around to warn them of what happens next.

"It falls to us to find a way to cross the Wailing Pass. The road ahead is by no means easy. Never before has the Pass been travelled; we have never been asked to do it. Warriors, I ask you today what have you to say to this defiant pass." The men bellow at the mountain roaring their defiance. I continue, "If you find yourself in the great halls of your forbears with a table spread before you, the cold has claimed you, the elders have called you to their halls and I will personally hold you on a charge. But if you are still with us when you reach the crest of the Pass you will have forever carved your name in the scrolls of honour. So what are we waiting for? Prepare to climb the Pass!" I shout, rattling my spear against my shield defying the power of the mountain. Men have been cheering all through my speech. Now it overflows into all the men cheering and bellowing. They shout to each other and clash their shield and spears together, ready to make this hard journey. The Battle Master takes control and sends the warriors back into the convoy ready to make the push up the gorge.

In next to no time the haulers are ready at the wagons, the warriors are geared up and the whole convoy is eager to tackle the passage. I look behind, making sure all is ready and then nod to the Battle Master.

He salutes and turns on his heel to face the muster. "Muster...Open formation...Move." There is the clank of chain mail and harnesses as the warriors take up their new positions ensuring there is enough space for the wagons to manoeuvre on the hill. The Battle Master nods, approving the execution of the formation change. He then inhales deeply and in parade ground style delivery, orders the muster forward. We march as one, in perfect step and pace. The entrance is narrow, it twists and turns making it hard to see ahead. The snow looks firm but it needs sounding. I tell the Battle Master to halt the company and take the twins up ahead to try the snow. Most of the men move closer to the wagons, sheltering them from the weather that seems to be worsening, the wind picking up and the clouds coming over fast. Once all is ready the muster rolls forward again. I hear the grunts of the haulers change as their workload increases as the ground starts to slope, I hear the wagon masters encourage them with a song and praise. The wind howls down at us as if trying to blow us back. It ferociously attacks our cloaks, whipping them around and flinging snow up into our eyes, making us squint and nearly blind. The sheer moan of the wind is fantastic. I am next to Yĭ-ăn-nī but I can barely hear him shout. We struggle up the pass and turn the corner to find the next passage. For what seems a lifetime, we struggle on. I look back over my shoulder and can just make out the leading wagon behind us. I turn my face back to the wind looking ahead into the gloom trying to sound the passage ahead. The wind is moaning louder than ever, and is also far colder than we have experienced before. The cold bites us even through the extra layers that were issued before the climb. Before long we are numb to all feeling. The wind has robbed the very warmth of our blood. The snow grows deeper and feels more like small sharp crystals than the soft snow of winter. This snow was not born on the wind and blown down from the clouds but fell on the mountain peaks and froze, its sides becoming sharp and stiff. It must then have fallen down the mountain or been pushed by a snow floods. A potential danger strikes, my mind and I turn to Yĭ-ăn-nī desperate for him to hear what I have to say. I pull him close and bellow down his ear, "Tell the men to keep quiet and tread carefully. A wrong move could make the snow run. Also check on the haulers; we will need to rotate them allowing them to rest, take some of the mountain warriors to help." He nods and turns aside to await the Battle Master to bring up some help. I turn back into the wind. The snow whips up and lodges in my beard, making my face cold from the touch of ice on my skin. Desperate for my body to remain warm, I knock the snow from my face and wrap my scarf around it, making it harder for the snow to stick. I shout behind me to Yă-nnī to move forward and take the lead giving me some time out of the full rage of the wind. Behind us there is a commotion and to my horror I see the first wagon slow to a halt and then begin to slip back. I plunge back down the pass and start racing towards the wagon closely followed by Yĭ-ăn-nī and Yă-nnī. We plunge down the path, forcing the snow apart and send it wildly into the air as we thunder past. By the time we have reached the wagon, it is sliding back down the Passage dragging all the haulers with it. On the bench, the wagon master is looking pale and he clings to the brake trying to slow the wagon. Next to him sits Kă-llī-ōpē clinging to the bench looking towards me with fear in her eyes. Her face is pale and she looks terrified. I feel a new energy course through my blood. As the wagon slides down, it sends the warriors left and right. I roar to the haulers to hold tight and send Kē-phās to grab a wheel and stop it sliding while I block the other. The gap between the wagons is shrinking fast, so the haulers let the other wagon roll back carefully to give us more room. I throw myself behind the groaning wheel, desperate to stop it. Kă-llī-ōpē leans over and watches me. I shout to her to leap off and with wild recklessness she throws herself into the snow banks. Glad to have her safe, I focus on saving the wagon. I groan and strain trying to stop the wagon from sliding any further. My feet scrabble trying to find a firm foothold to push. I keep sliding backwards, unable to halt the wagon, the weight is just too much and the footholds too loose.

I look desperately from side to side, trying to tip the balance back to our favour and wrestle victory from the ice.

I shout out to no one and yet everyone, "Form a wall behind the wagon. Use the heavy spears to brace yourselves." There is a flurry of activity as men hurl past me, eager to join the wall rapidly forming behind the wagon. I close my eyes trying to focus all my strength trying to halt this wagon. There is a jolt as the wagon hits the wall and then with a gentle slowing the wagon halts. I open my eyes, nod to the wagon master who breathes deeply and wipes his face on his sleeve.

I indulge the men, letting them cheer. "That's enough. Do you want to be over this wall by nightfall or sleeping on the ice? Battle Master fetch out the ice shoes." The Battle Master nods and turns to the wagons to unload the iron-shod shoes that provide good grip for climbers.

I turn back to the men. "This time we are going to take it slowly. There will be a team of six haulers pulling and then there will be five mountain warriors behind providing a brake wall." Once all is prepared I give the all clear sign to the Battle Master who bellows the command to move forward. After waiting for the first wagon to begin rolling, the Battle Master, satisfied with the large gap between the two wagons again, gives the signal to start the second wagon rolling.

We struggle up two more corridors, the track becoming steeper. We reach the next corner and turn it. Ahead the passage widens into a clearing where the snow lies flat. We stop here the exhausted haulers collapsing in the snow. I call together the more senior officers for a plan of action. "We must continue to advance but the snow is becoming deeper and our troops are becoming weaker. We need ideas, what have we got to use?" I pace in the snow, waiting for suggestions. Nīk-ă-tōr steps forward, "the wagons can be fitted with skis to help them over the deeper snow." I nod, holding the idea, waiting for more information to make the plan clearer. The senior war gang master steps forward, "the warriors can last a lot longer if they can have a good break." I nod adding this detail to the mix. "We carry ropes and timbers, we can use them to anchor the wagons and stop them rolling back." The wagon master speaks up. "Good thinking we can use that. But oh wait, wait," I stop mid pace, as my mind combines the facts and the fog lifts. The answer is simple. "This is the solution. We shall take the mountain warriors ahead with the timbers and rope. We shall set up a pulley and haul the wagons up length by length of the passage. The wind warriors and haulers will follow up behind to act as a fail-safe. Any questions?" There are nods and murmurs of approval to my plan, "Then let us be about our business."

The group breaks up and everyone moves to his post. I detail the wind warriors to remain on guard and order the column to fall in and follow. By the time we move across the clearing and prepare to march up the next part of the passage, the haulers are already fitting the skis to the wagons. Before we move off a group of warriors run up to us carrying the rope and timbers to make the pulley. "We shall attempt an easy pull first." I instruct the other Royal Guards. We throw ourselves at the passage again, and start climbing. I mentally count off one hundred and fifty paces then call a halt. We find part of the passage that is flat and large enough to hold the wagons and I order the warriors to deploy the equipment just beyond the staging area. Up go the timbers, the pulley is hung and the rope is slung over ready to heave up the wagons. The warriors fall in and I give the rope a tug. It feels securely tied to the other end and I feel somebody answer my tug. "Battle Master, in your own time." He nods and turns to the lines of warriors. "Brace, and heave. One, two, one, two. Keep pulling. Do not slack." Up comes the first wagon. Once it reaches the flat, the rope is unhooked and a warrior is given the rope to take back down to the second wagon. Before long the second wagon is with us and we are all assembled. Yĭ-ăn-nī walks over to me, saying, "It seems this plan works the best."

"Good," I answer "because we must have countless more stages ahead of us. Time to walk the next phase."

On we struggle against storm and blizzard. We battle on against the wind, pushing further and further up the Wailing Pass. Sometimes the wind seems to be winning, forcing us back and throwing us back down the Pass. Then the wind blows itself out and we make good head-way, forging our way up the hill. Snow and stone cannot hold us back as we push on. Then the wind regroups and again blows down at us. It slows our progress as we face renewed snow gales. My scarf is wound tightly round my face leaving only a small slot for my eyes. Not that I can see much with the wind driving the snow around me. The wind pushes down on me all the harder and the only way I can forge ahead is to turn sideways and edge forward, feeling my way using the points of my feet. It is a constant battle just to swing one foot in front of the other. The snow storm presses closer as if moving in for the kill, I though the weather was bad before but now it is terrible. I can barely see an arm's length ahead of me. I look behind me and all I can see is the dim outline of Kē-phās behind.

I pull him close and shout in his ear, "Pass the word for the men to link spears. We do not want to lose anyone." He nods and swings round to pass the message on. While I wait for the message to relay, I grasp my spear near the tip, thrusting the shaft behind me to let Kē-phās hold on. The shaft jars as Kē-phās grips it. I shake the spear and begin pushing forward once again. Now I have no way of feeling the path ahead and I have to edge forward, sliding my feet along. Always the slope leads steeply up, we seem to have spent most of our time climbing and I wonder for at least the tenth time how high and far we have climbed and more importantly, how far do we have still to go? And still the slope becomes steeper; the men are exhausted with pulling the wagons up the passage. After the fifteenth passage we reach another open plaza and stop for a rest. The cold soon drives us on. It is both an ally and enemy. The cold stops our hands hurting from the rope burns and cuts but it also forces us to keep moving in case it chills us too much and steals our breath away.

The cold is biting, the wind is roaring, the snow is swirling and time is running out. The more the weather oppresses, the more pressure is put on us. Even the formidable army training of our warriors cannot help us last forever. If we are forced to stop we shall freeze, our bodies lost in the snow and our mission unfulfilled. This danger forces us on. My feet already feel like blocks of ice, heavy and numbed; it requires all of my will to keep them moving. I struggle forward with the snow up to my knees. Eventually it proves too much and as my foot jams under the snow, I stumble. Forward I fall, but instead of my face being planted in snow, I land on my knees with my face still being whipped by the wind. My heart skips a beat. Can it be possible? I eagerly pull myself to my feet and move forward, taking my spear from Kē-phās' hand. The ground is flat. I use my spear to try to find where slope starts again, but all I can feel is flat land. We have reached the top.

CHAPTER 7

I SHOUT WITH PURE uncontrolled joy. I turn back and jump back down over the crest, colliding with Kē-phās and sending us both sprawling on the snow. To make matters more complicated the warriors directly behind Kē-phās do not react quick enough and in turn also trip over us adding to the confusion. This brings the whole marching column to a halt as we disentangle ourselves.

I feel my head going light and struggle to breathe with the weight of bodies above me pushing me down into the snow. I hear shouting and the weight begins to shift. Hands grip my arms and pull me up. I rise, gasping for air enjoying the taste of the fresh cold air that only moments ago had been burning my chest. I gasp trying to tell someone what is awaiting us.

I grab Kē-phās by his cloak and shout in his ear, "We are near the top, we've done it." Within minutes the whole column is buzzing with excitement. The cold is forgotten, the wind seems to die down, then snow no longer bites. The mere chance of success has brought hope and new energy.

"Come, let us seal our victory over this Pass." I spat contemptuously. The men who can hear me cheer and with me leading they surge on over the head of the Wailing Pass and out of the snow storm into a light mist. At first there is sheer exhilaration at having conquered the heights of the Wailing Pass. Then thoughts turn to more practical matters. Warriors pile their shields and weapons to help the labourers pull the wagons for the final time.

In next to no time the Battle Master has organized the tripods and ropes. While Nīk-ă-tōr and his fellow surveyors pull out their maps to continue their work, I lend a hand to pull the wagons up. Calling time the Battle Master walks up and down, eager to make sure everyone is trying. Here and there he shouts louder to deliver encouragement. With squeals and much groaning the first wagon is hauled up. One of the haulers unhooks the wagon and slides back down the hill to fix the second wagon on. Meanwhile the warriors rest and begin a hubbub of chattering. I over hear one of the younger wind warriors talking to scarred veteran War Gang Master.

"What do you reckon we shall find?" asks the younger.

"I do not know. There could be Night Shadows, ghosts, even giant men here" replies the War Gang Master, casually stirring a stew pot full of rapidly melting snow. The younger looks worried and glances around him pulling cloak around himself trying to hide his shivers. At this point the Battle Master, bustles up to check on the stew. "What rubbish is he pouring into your ear? I warned you before, sergeant about scaring the women." Trying not to make it obvious that I am listening I edge closer, smirking at the customary name for the wind warriors. The young warrior repeats the War Gang Master's taunts who is staring into the pot with a grin.

The Battle Master smiles "Do not let this scaremonger make you nervous. He is as nervous as you. Just remember your training and you will do fine. Time to fall back in." The hauler has returned to bring the second wagon up. The other warriors are already taking their places.

After rigging the tents and a hot meal of stew, most of the warriors fall into sleep, apart from those who have to mount the first watch. I do not envy them their task, to fall asleep on duty is bring disgrace on all and to face certain punishment. I am happy to let my head fall on my cloak and let sleep overtake me. I drift off to sleep, warm and content. I wake in a cold sweat and breathing heavily, trying to throw the images of nightmares out of my head and memory. Around me the other guards rumble in their sleep and rather than risking waking one of them, I quietly steal of out the tent for some fresh air. Once outside in the early morning sun I walk out of the camp barely acknowledging the watches' salute. Instead I leave the camp and make for an out crop that has appeared out of the receding fog since yesterday.

The morning cold nips at my face and fingers, by the time I scramble to the top of the rock, I am already feeling the cold. I sit down, pulling my cloak around me and staring at the snow before me. I wish the cold could numb my mind and distract me from my thoughts. Ideas blizzard me, threatening to snow flood my mind. Round and round run the questions. Who dared to break our peace? Who could have waited in ambush and then coldly displaced the convoy? Could they have even been human? Surely not, given the brutality. Where are the younger members of the convoy, the children and young? How could they have killed some of our finest warriors? So engrossed in my thoughts am I that I do not notice the crunch of snow behind me. A shadow falls across me and instantly I am on a war footing. I throw myself off the stone not looking back. Rolling in the snow I scramble to my feet. Braced for combat I look back, only to see Kă-llī-ōpē standing near the rock, smiling.

"You creep like the night."

She smiles, "It is easy to creep up on distracted people." I smile at the quote from the Elders' knowledge. "Something troubles you?" she asks.

"I was unable to sleep. I had a lot on my mind. I am still troubled." I confess looking down, observing proper protocol for single women. She smiles at my formality, "Does that mask ever slip, I wonder?"

I look straight at her momentarily, breaking the protocol and looking her square in the eye." It does not often break. I am worried of late and prefer my own council." I concede. It takes all my will to tear my eyes away and observe the proper respect.

She smiles and tilts her head, looking at me, trying to understand. "Why do men always hide their feelings and thoughts, it disturbs them more? Nīk-ă-tōr was like this for a long time after his loss."

Surprised at her forwardness, I recall the song of Hy-pă-tōs, the Life of Man. I try to explain, stopping often to choose my words, "When you build your life with someone and come to rely on them, it can make a man strong. You tend to be weaker if you lose those you hold dear. You no longer have a purpose. The only way a man can deal with that is to hide and live his life with ghosts. He tends to live the rest of his existence going through the motions of life, but his heart is long since dead, like flower cut from a plant."

Kă-llī-ōpē frowns, her brow creasing, trying to understand this argument from the other side of the stockade. I watch her face, trying to read her thoughts, surprisingly easy now she seems distracted, or is she toying with me? She seems to decide on an argument and begins it. "A flower when replanted can become alive again. It can grow roots and start again once more."

I nod, trying to predict her next attack, "Yes a flower can, but only if it wants to. If it has lost its will then there is no chance."

"And what would it take to put the will back into the flower?" she eyes with a twinkle in her eye. I notice her move carefully down the rock she sits on, I do not move away as tradition would demand.

"The prospect of starting again and becoming much greater than before." I answer finally understanding the game she plays with me. My heart skips a beat and I look up to find her watching me her head tilted. Her face seems so close as she sits just above me. That perfect face...I dare not believe she would consider.

She raises an eyebrow a playful smile on her lips, "Why so serious and cold?"

My control over my face abandons me and my face cracks into a nervous smile unable to conceal my joy anymore. She seems surprised and blushes, her cheeks turning a deep crimson. I realize the foolishness of it all, both of us so nervous and yet so confident, unable to have the courage to say precisely what we mean and having to use a flower to make our meaning clear. I throw my head back, laughing loud and clear. She watches me, my sudden change wrong footing her and throwing her balance. Then the humour hits her and she smiles. The smile widens and splits, revealing perfectly set white teeth and she laughs. We both laugh together, me falling back in the snow unable to remain upright. She struggles to keep her seat and ends up falling off it into the thick carpet of snow. I stop laughing looking at her lying in the snow laughing, her beauty shining like a star on a dark night.

I summon my courage; taking a deep breathe I edge forward, "You are more beautiful than a summer's day or the bloom of a flower." She smiles, tossing her hair and fluttering her eyes. It is enough to stop my heart and I am struck dumb. She is beautiful and she knows it. She ought not to be let out alone.

She opens her eyes wide and sit up with a smile, "Why young Man? Is that an offer of Binding?"

I smile and bow, responding with the traditional answer, "Well young Lady if your bloodline can spare you and you consent to the Bind." I take a deep breath, hoping for the traditional reply.

She watches me and then sits up straight, tossing her hair defiantly, "How could a young Lady refuse such an offer from a noble warrior." With that she sits forward and grips my hand. The touch of her skin sets my heart beating fast and I turn my hand to hold her wrist gently trying not to hurt her.

"You took your time asking. I was being to wonder if you liked someone else." She murmurs.

The sound of whistling makes us both start and pull apart. Nīk-ă-tōr is standing on top of the rock clapping and grinning madly, "Tisk, Tisk. I trusted you, Kă-llī-ōpē, to behave when you came, I expected better than this, Āi-ās, being alone with an unbound woman." He says playfully mocking us. He then lets out a burst of laughter and jumps down the rocks, landing in the snow beside us and pulling us into an embrace. "Stop looking like scolded children and smile. I shall tell the Battle Master to prepare for the ceremony. I can also collect my winnings." He nudges me, "better make sure she does not leave."

"You do not think I would let her escape me do you?" I ask Kă-llī-ōpē simply smiles.

As we return to camp the sentries are being changed, the Battle Master walking the lines. He bows low to me, trying not to smile. I roll my eyes, "Battle Master, if you are not too busy would you prepare a binding ceremony for mid-morning muster?"

He bows low, trying desperately to hide his smile, "Whom is the ceremony for?"

"Why, do not you know?" I say looking startled, "And I was informed you had an interest in relation to this alliance."

The smile finally breaks, "I shall make all the arrangements." He replies and turns to Nīk-ă-tōr. "I shall tell the wagon master to make the arrangements."

"Ah yes! I must attend to the item we discussed", replies Nīk-ă-tōr. With that they both bow and leave, walking quickly to attend their business.

"Well it appears we are left alone." I turn to Kă-llī-ōpē.

"Well actually I must take my leave of you; I have to make preparations of my own." smiles Kă-llī-ōpē.

With that she turns and leaves me standing in the camp, my mouth open. I turn to one of the sentries and roll my eyes. He smiles and half bows towards me. I return to my tent to polish my armour and clean my clothes.

Inside the tent I see Kē-phās sitting by the fire. I nod to him then sit by the fire near my armour, pulling a bowl of oil close. I settle down, take up the rag, dip a corner in the oil and take up my breast plate and then it dawns on me.

"I am being bound," I say in a voice of wonder, not wanting to believe this change of circumstances.

Kē-phās pulls me from my dreams, "What was that?"

My face cracks into a grin from one ear to the other "Hear my news and sing with me for today I am to be bound and my blood group will survive another generation."

Without hesitation, Kē-phās jumps up, shouting happiness and bellowing with all his voice. Around me other warriors jump up, shouting their happiness. They begin crowding round asking details. I hold my hands up, "I have to be ready by morning muster." They begin to disperse, each talking rapidly the excitement, growing quickly.

The time seems to drag slowly. I rub down my armour until the fire glints in it. Around me the world seems to move painfully slow. The more I want it to go fast, the slower it goes. Everyone around me is busy and I have nothing to do. Instead I am happy to sit and wonder at what is about to happen.

Overhead the sun climbs higher until it reaches the midday mark. Across the camp horns break out, but today the notes are different; on top of the changing of the guard is a new tune, which breaks my thoughts and throws me into action. The tent is deserted but I do not really notice. Typical. The one day I must be on time and I am late. I hurriedly pull on my armour, hopping towards the door. I reach the flap and click my fingers in annoyance turning back to grab my spear. I hurry through the camp, dodging around the wagon and racing round the fire. On and on I rush towards the far side of the camp sliding to a stop in the snow, as I round a tent.

Ahead of me I can see the guard of honour, 20 warriors in two ranks their spears grounded shields slung loose. I breathe deep to ease my racing heart and face up my armour and cloak, brushing a stray snowflake from my arm. I lean my spear against my side and push my arm through my shield slings. I take a last look over my helmet using the reflection to run a hand through my hair and to tweak my beard. I then slide my helmet on visor down, take up my spear, then stand still. The Battle Master, who has been watching, taps his staff on the ground and the warriors raise their spears, shields and stand to attention. The Battle Master looks over the ranks making sure all is perfect and raises his staff to point at me. I raise my head and dip it slightly in acknowledgement and begin to march forward slowly and carefully, trying hard not to upset my cloak which billows behind me in the gentle breeze.

As I make my way to the Battle Master, the warriors bow low as I pass by, timing it perfectly with the warrior opposite them, but I do not have eyes for them. In fact what I have eyes for and what my heart yearns for cannot be seen. Kă-llī-ōpē and Nīk-ă-tōr will approach after me. I reach the Battle Master and take my place to his left, still facing him. I hand my shield and spear to his War Gang Master who offers me a grin. I pull my helmet off and tuck it under my arm. I turn back to the Battle Master who bows to me and I return it, then freeze in place as he raises his staff again and points it behind me. I hear the clank of armour as the guards stand to attention as Kă-llī-ōpē begins her approach, on the arm of Nīk-ă-tōr. I dare not look as some believe it bad luck. I hear the snow crunch behind me gently and I see the Battle Master smile and then she arrives. I valiantly keep my eyes pinned forward but can hardly resist the urge to look at her.

Dressed in a white cloak trimmed with fur, her deep hood is up, preventing me from seeing her face. As she stands beside me I feel light headed and my heart seems ready to burst. I almost have to pinch myself to make sure I am not dreaming. But then the battle master makes it real. He bows to both me and Kă-llī-ōpē and then instructs us to face one another. I take a step back and spin on my ankle to face Kă-llī-ōpē. She very gracefully turns to face me her cloak catching the wind and flowing out behind her. I can still not see her face as she keeps her hood up. The Battle Master begins to speak, but my attention is not on him until I hear my name. "Āi-ās, Heir of Stră-thōn, Son of the Ă-kay-dăs do you swear to be loyal to your woman as long as your life breath is within? Are you willing to defend her honour even unto death?"

Without pause I answer "I, Āi-ās, Heir of Stră-thōn, Son of the Ă-kay-dăs do swear this. I would willingly give my life for hers."

The Battle Master nods and turns to Kă-llī-ōpē, "Are you willing to bind yourself to this Son of Ă-kay-dăs until either one of you is called to the table of the Elders?"

A voice issues from the hood, clear as crystal, "I willingly do so."

He nods to Nīk-ă-tōr who has been standing behind us. Nīk-ă-tōr walks to Kă-llī-ōpē obstructing my view of her. He lowers her hood and kisses her on the forehead, giving her his blessing. He then bows to her and moves back. What a sight I see! Kă-llī-ōpē has indeed been busy. Her silvery hair is braided and hooped around her ears. It is pulled back from her face and over her forehead she wears a pendant. After this day she shall not wear her hair loose in public as an un-partnered woman. Her face is smoothed and fine, pale as silver but contrasted by her flushed cheeks and yet that is not what awes me most. Her lips are painted a deep crimson, beautifully contrasting her skin and yet these do not fascinate me. It is her eyes, those large orbs so clear and calm, palest blue and yet so powerful and gripping. She sees my attention and her blushes deepen. Nīk-ă-tōr allows me to continue to gaze upon her for a while longer then again steps forward, a piece of cord in his hand. He holds his hand out for Kă-llī-ōpē's hand and mine. He gently takes her arm and holds it face up he then puts my arm on top facing downward. He then binds our arms together as a sign that we have been bound together for all time. All the time we have never taken our eyes off each other.

Now the Battle Master takes over, "Man is to guard his woman from all danger, this is why your hand is above, Āi-ās. Woman is to support her man in any way she can. Neither of you are in control; you must work together. You must love one another and give for what you take. Long live Āi-ās and Kă-llī-ōpē. Long may the Elders honour and watch you." Then Nīk-ă-tōr unbinds our arms. However as the cord falls away Kă-llī-ōpē seems unwilling to let my hand go...not that I am complaining. "As is customary Āi-ās you are relieved of your duties for the remainder of this day, I suggest that you spend it wisely."

As his words die down the camp erupts into cheers and blaring horns. Now the celebration can begin. The warriors form a tunnel of spears for us to walk down and both of us break into smiles. Ahead of us walk the hornists, sounding long low songs of celebration on their instruments. Around us the other warriors cheer and clash their spears together. All around us shouts of encouragement can be heard. I look back to Nīk-ă-tōr who has tears in his eyes and is smiling, wildly happy. I feel exuberant and like a child, again such is my happiness. I step forward mischievously and half turn back to Kă-llī-ōpē, "May I be permitted to walk you back to camp?"

Kă-llī-ōpē smiles her eye shining, "It is best so. These warriors may try to steal me away."

"Let them try." I reply and put my arm around her shoulders. She puts her arms around me and to my utter surprise kisses me. I freeze with shock and around me there are whistles and various shouts. I sweep her up into my arms, lifting her clear off the floor, settling her against my chest. The warriors go wild and there is more cheering as I walk down the ranks holding my heart in my arms.

Next comes our first act as newly paired, building our tent. The spectators chase us as we go the open section of the camp site where we shall build our tent. To much merriment and laughter, eventually the tent is built and we are able to go inside and shut the world out. I stretch out on the ground and rest, to be joined by my woman. Time seems to pass quickly and before we realize it the evening horns are calling. I put my head out of the tent in disbelief, but it is true the sun is falling and the shadows are growing longer. I sit back beside Kă-llī-ōpē and sigh long and loud. Kă-llī-ōpē sits up, resting on her elbow, "What?" she asks.

"This morning I was awake early worrying about what happens next. I was the last of my bloodline with no partner and I was almost out of hope. Now it is the end of the day, I have a woman, who is beautiful, wise, and kind!" I reply as Kă-llī-ōpē stretches.

"Do not let me stop you! I believe you were going to say happy, good with food, strong!" she helpfully suggests.

I laugh and poke her in the ribs, making her giggle.

That night as I drift off to sleep, listening to Kă-llī-ōpē's shallow breathing beside me, I wonder at it all, how a man's fortune can change in the space of one day. That night my dreams do not trouble me. The world seems back in balance and pulling itself back together. But it will not last. The Great Evil, now awake, prepares to move again.

I awake to the sound of morning horns. Beside me I hear movement and freeze reaching for my spear. Then I remember and smile, rolling over and coming face to face with those pale blue eyes. I smile distracted, almost mesmerised by the power in those eyes. Kă-llī-ōpē smiles and twitches her nose. The horn sounds again and she looks towards the doorway, "Should you answer that, you only had one day's break."

I roll my eyes and sit up, "Huh, she's already trying to be rid of me." I say to no one in particular. I stand up and stretch groaning loudly, watching Kă-llī-ōpē wince as my shoulders creak. I stand tall and stretch again, then pull on my clothes and armour, sling my cloak around my shoulders and with a final farewell leave the tent, entering the cool morning mist.

Around me the camp is stirring, the sentinels are changing and the camp preparing for a new day. The wagon haulers, led by a Wagon Master, take a boiling pot of food around the tents, dispensing the rations that will fuel the first part of the day. As I watch they reach the last tent and after serving food return towards the wagon. The Wagon Master nods to the Battle Master, who raises his horn and blows three notes. The hubbub in the tents increase as the warriors prepare for morning inspection. I walk across the camp, acknowledging the salutes of the sentinels and making my way towards the Battle Master, who smiles and wishes me good day. He gives me the morning report and then awaits the day's instructions.

After a brief thought and look around I begin, "This morning I want the camp dismantled and ready to move before the sun rises high. We shall move further from the ridge. We shall need scouts as we have no knowledge of what could be waiting us. That is all." We exchange salutes and go our separate ways. I meet Nīk-ă-tōr and talk with him for a while until the horn sounds again; two blasts this time. I make my excuses and return to the tent finding that food has been delivered and is steaming gently, Kă-llī-ōpē is dressed and just about to start. Before long the horns sounds again, one long blast as we finish our food, and we both leave the tent making our way to where the warriors are forming up ready for morning parade. Kă-llī-ōpē slips her arm through mine and we walk together to the centre of the camp.

Warriors are piling out of their tents forming ranks and all under the watchful gaze of the Battle Master. He watches with pride as the warriors form up and neaten their lines. Once assembled and the last line jostled into place, the inspection begins. As Royal Guards we are the only military force exempt from such parades, being senior to any other warrior. We do however watch them, making sure all is done according to lore and tradition. The Battle Master begins to walk the lines, tapping his staff on the ground as he goes. He looks at armour, shield, spear and warrior, making sure all are properly cared for. He walks the length of the front line then crisply turns at the end of the line to walk back along the second. Once he finishes his inspection, he marches up to his place in the line and freezes. Then in a voice that cuts through the mist and rings around the camp, calls the muster to attention and salutes, handing the parade to me. I step forward, leaving Kă-llī-ōpē, to address the muster.

"Today we will begin to map this area for our Supreme Ruler. I was impressed by your conduct on the Wailing Pass. I cannot say what we shall find but I have every confidence in your abilities. You shall have drill manoeuvre and inspections, until we are ready to depart. Muster...Re align ranks...Stand tall. Battle Master carry on with combat practise." With that I turn on my heel and walk towards the other Royal Guards who are awaiting instructions for the day. I offer Kă-llī-ōpē my arm as the warriors split into pairs to practise. The Battle Master begins to sing the warrior's chant.

Show them iron,
Show them bone,
Take them down to graves of stone,

Show them spear,
Show no tear,
Show them that we cannot fear.

"Good morning, today we shall be advancing north to find what this place holds for us. I want the camp dismantled and ready to move by mid-day. Anyone with questions?" No one makes a move, "Excellent. Be about your businesses."

I leave the group still with Kă-llī-ōpē on my arm. I feel her shiver in the morning crisp air and pat her hand reassuringly. Nīk-ă-tōr hails us, joining us; we walk around the camp talking about the day ahead. By time we have finished the circuit the inspection is over and formation practise is taking place. We stop to watch the warriors in action. The warriors stand in their groups the three Mountain warriors in the centre, the two Wind warriors at each end of the line. The mountain warriors stand their spears on the floor keeping them close to their shields ensuring they will not hurt anyone. The Wind warriors stand easy with spears held rigidly at their sides. The Battle Master hits the earth with his spear butt, making a dull thud. "Heavy Muster form ranks...Prepare to form shield wall...On my command...form." The first rank of Mountain warriors crouch low holding their spears out only an arm's length off the Ground. The second rank lift their shields over the front ranks head and thrust their spears forward over their shields. Once still, all the warriors clang their shields together to make sure they are all connected. Smooth and precise, this is a well-trained War Band. "Shield Wall...Half speed forward." The wall begins to edge forward, the senior War Gang Master calling the paces. "Shield Wall...Break and Charge." Gone is the formation, with a roar and clattering of shields the first rank spring up and run forward followed; by the other ranks. Shield held forward, spear held low ready to stab forward and up under shield and armour. The weight of the charge will be enough to crush anyone stuck in the way. "Halt...Form up, form ranks." Instantly the charge is brought under control, the warriors stop and shuffle their ranks. The Battle Master nods, pleased with their efforts. He gives the warriors a moment to catch their breath and reform their ranks. He praises them for their work and drill.

He then turns his attention to the wind warriors who have been standing to one side. It is their turn to test their drill. But first he needs to set the battle. He turns back to the Mountain warriors and orders them to form a shield wall. Once they are in formation he begins. "Light Muster, form up." The wind warriors take their places in two ranks deep, behind the warriors well-spaced apart to make sure they have enough room. They stand easy waiting for the next command. "Light Muster, prepare." The wind warriors raise their small shields and spears. "Light Muster, prepare to let fly." They swing their shields over their shoulders letting them hang so they do not hinder their arms. Spears gripped in an over arm grip, points near the ground. "Light Muster, let fly." Back go the arms, spear tips swinging towards the sky. A moment of rest, stillness before the activity. Then with a grunt, the wind warriors run forward two paces to swing the spear forward and send it sailing on its way. Over the heads of the mountain warriors and then thirty paces more to land quivering in the ground. "Light Muster tally-ho." With a cheer the wind warriors stream around the sides of the mountain warriors. The Battle Master is obviously pleased with the demonstration of his troops. He calls them together to congratulate them; we turn away as the camp is broken up and loaded back on the wagons.

As the light grows, we form up ready to move on. The last of the camp is loaded on the wagons and the warriors take their places in the convoy. Two war gangs of Mountain warriors at the front of the convoy, the two war gangs of Wind warriors placed in-between the wagons and the remaining War Gang of Mountain warrior placed at the rear. After inspecting the convoy, I nod my approval to the Battle Master and join the other Royal Guards at the front. The mist still swirls around but seems to be thinning. Yă-nnī, Yĭ-ăn-nī and Nīk-ă-tōr each take two mountain warriors as escorts then take their places ahead of the column to act as scouts, with orders to return if they meet anything. They disappear into the mists, Yă-nnī going to the left, Yĭ-ăn-nī going to the right and Nīk-ă-tōr taking the centre. I give them a moment to get up ahead, then I order the column to fall in and advance. The snow is thick underfoot and we march slowly as the wagon haulers struggle on. We make good progress, the ground levels out more and the wind begins to blow. The sun becomes clearer as it climbs higher in the sky.

The mists still swirl round making it hard for us to see anything, with a screech and a groan the lead wagon tumbles into a patch of deep snow, forcing the soldiers to stop. Under the pressure the wheel cracks and it takes a long time to dig the wagon out and change the wheel. In the meantime, a fire is started using up some of the precious fuel, food is cooked and water boiled to help the warriors warm up. We are just finishing our meal when one of Nīk-ă-tōr's Warriors come jogging up the path.

He runs up to where we are sitting and falls on his knees before us. He makes to speak but I motion for him to catch his breath. He breathes deeply, letting his heart slow. "Captain, up ahead the mist is thicker and there are many dark shapes. We cannot tell properly where one stops and another begins." While he is still talking a warrior sent by Yĭ-ăn-nī bounds through the snow and even a warrior from Yă-nnī appears, all reporting the same information. I sit on the ground listening to all the reports, only interrupting to ask an occasional question. Kē-phās watches me. I rest my chin on my upturned hands while I form a solution, then I sit forward. "You will return to your war gangs." I turn and shout for a hornists. "Sound the recall for the scouts." As the hornist begins to sound the recall, I call the Battle Master over. "Form the warriors into a battle line. Bring up the colour War Gang and keep the formation close. We are moving to a war footing." The Battle Master nods then turns aside taking his place at the head of the column to begin forming the battle line. "Muster...hear and heed. We are moving to a war footing. Muster will form column to the side of the wagon in preparation to form line. Muster form up." The warriors wait for a heartbeat, then spin on their heels to their left and then move ten paces. They then turn right and freeze, facing forward. The battle master nods and begins the next phase. "Muster...War gangs one, three and five form the first line. War gangs two and four will form second line. Colour gang will form behind gang three. Muster on my mark...Form." The warriors all stand straight, then begin to move. The first gang move left, the fifth gang move right and the third gang move forward to take the centre. The colour gang move forward, their standards still encased and protected. Gang two and four from line behind the other gangs. The gangs freeze and stand still. The battle master nods and turns back to me. "Permission to move the wagons into formation and unfurl the standards?" I gesture for him to continue.

He turns back to the developing formation, "Wagon muster form line behind the warrior muster." The wagons haulers strain to pull the wagons into position. The colour party are now in position. "Muster will move to a war footing, War Gang Masters to centre front, weapon casings off. Move up." I watch carefully, noting the War Gang Masters, large veteran fighters selected to command the war gangs, take their places in the front rank of their warriors. These men are tall and strong. Showing no fear or emotion, they are expected to lead their men come what may. They carry the evidence of a life as a warrior; scars and a grim presence that holds most raw recruits in awe. No one would call them handsome for all their scarring, but there is something in them that men look up to. There is a respect and trust that comes easily to them for their life of service. They carry their weapons lightly, a testament to their skill and strength. They are men of stone.

The lines open to allow the masters to take their place, then close and realign their formations. I leave Kă-llī-ōpē at the wagon after squeezing her hand gently. I walk through the formation to take my place to the left of the colour squad as the most senior officer. The battle master takes his place next to me and freezes in place ready for the next command, happy with his execution of my orders. All around there is silence; after the jangling of harnesses and metal it sounds strange. I give the ranks a moment to breathe while I plan my next move. There is one final task to do before the formation is ready to march into the unknown. The Standards must be unfurled.

"Colour Gang, prepare to let fly." The Colour guards, heavily armoured veteran warriors guarding the heart of the War Band, raise the tightly bound standards ready to release them, ready to loose the heart of war. I raise my spear ready to sound the advance. "Let fly the heart of war, let fly the sound of war. Loose the warrior's heart." The veterans release the knots and the heavy folds of the standards shake themselves free. Released from their knots they fly in the wind. We are ready for war. "Advance!" I bellow.

The mists swirl and the wind blows, the metal clanks and the standards flap as we march to war. As we march forward we meet the other Royal Guards who report shapes in the mists up ahead. In accordance with scouting rules they stopped and waited. I raise my fist and the formation halts. "Where precisely are the shapes?" I ask the guards, not wanting to advance further until the information is clearer. Nīk-ă-tōr steps forward, "Ahead the mists are thinner and the ground climbs to a ledge. In the mists many dark moving shapes can be seen but there is not enough cover to move forward and acquire a clearer picture." The other guards agree. "The movement is strange however, the shapes do not seem to go anywhere just move back and forth." Yĭ-ăn-nī adds. Whatever is awaiting us is presenting a large front. The warriors around us fidget, wanting to move on, and a War Gang Master snaps a rebuke. I decide on a course of action. "Advance half pace." The Senior War Gang Master calls the timing and again we move forward on full alert.

Before long we reach the ridge and the mists thin to reveal very tall moving shapes. I call a halt, and the formation once more grinds to a halt. "Battle Master will take charge. Royal Guards will follow me. We shall investigate." We march forward and I feel a shiver run across my spine at leaving the protection of the warriors. We walk forward up the slope and all the time the shapes in the mists become more defined, clearer. The dark shapes seem to sway all the time growing taller and bigger. The wind whips over the snow, making the shapes blurred.

The shapes continue to emerge out of the snow, and as they become clear, I turn and shout, grinning happily. We have succeeded and there is hope for our people yet. For the giant shapes are pine trees, a whole forest of them as far as the eye can see. Yă-nnī looks at the trees and in a faraway voice comments, "There are more than enough trees to keep our people warm for ever." He walks up to trees, eyes fixed on them in wonder and awe. He tentatively touches the trees as if worried they may vanish as a dream. But no, they remain. He tries to put his arms around the nearest and cannot link his fingers. I move in closer to the broad trunk and look up. The cloak of greenery only grows on the outside and I see right up the inside tree. Such a tangle of branches, I have never seen. Maybe more than fifty, many are thicker than my chest. "I am going to attempt to climb up and see what is beyond. While I am gone someone call up the army and bring them to the tree line." I drop my shield and spear, calling to Kē-phās to stand by the trunk under the lowest branch. I step back to let him take his place near the trunk. He then links his hands together and braces. I place my left foot in his hands after letting my coat of rings fall to the ground. The weight would bend the branches and make me too heavy. I marvel at the lightness after the heavy weight of the armour. I nod to Kē-phās and with a grunt he lifts me up to the lowest branch. I take a firm grip, then swinging my legs up I scramble ungainly onto the branch. I call down to say that I am going up further and hear Kă-llī-ōpē telling me to take care. The lowest branch was the hardest, the inside of the tree almost has steps where the branches are bare of twigs near the trunk. Below me someone sounds a horn and calls to the Battle Master to call up the warriors. The horn blast rings up the tree making the spikes quiver and the branches vibrate. Climbing the tree makes me hot, I find myself sweating and wishing I had left my cloak on the ground. I look down, intending to drop it down but give up when I see the tangle below. It does not take me long to reach what I think is the halfway point of the tree, although the branches are still thicker than my arms. I crouch on a solid one and work my way out to peer through the greenery. The spikes are thankfully blunt although they still poke. I work my way past them, conscious of the drop below me. The cold begins to bite as my head emerges into the fog. I gulp and grip tighter. I have come up much higher than I expected. Below me I see the others so small and far away. They notice me and wave; I dare not wave back. I try to look up but dare not turn too far, and only end up with a face full of spikes. Below me I hear the clank of armour and shield as the warriors approach. Out of the fog they come, standards flying, sun glinting on the polished shields, the warriors moving as one, I watch their approach until they halt at the tree line. I crawl back along my branch the spines swallowing me. I slither back down the tree and land on the ground with a crash.

The other guards are looking into the forest. They seem not notice my arrival. "Something wrong?" I query. Kă-llī-ōpē turns round and smiles to see me back, "After Yă-nnī sounded the advance, another trumpet call answered him. It was badly blown and was not an recognized call." She explains. "Surely it was just the echo, twisted by the pines. Ah, Battle Master, it seems we have solved the problem of fuel. Have scouts deploy in the pines to find a suitable place to establish a camp." I address the Battle Master who has joined our group from the waiting ranks of warriors.

The ranks of warriors stand still and silent. The Battle Master gives a curt order and the first two ranks of wind warriors uncover their spears, break ranks and run into the trees, scouting ahead. Meanwhile I talk to Kē-phās and Nīk-ă-tōr, "Put a War Gang Master under My-rōn and let him do some scouting. Put the wind warriors on guard duty, while the haulers establish a camp. Take one of the final Mountain Warrior squad and go out scouting. I shall take the final group and scout in a different direction. We have found a new home, let us see if it is worthy of us and what it can offer us."

A shout from one of the scouts instantly stops all conversation he comes hurtling back out of the tree line. After a brief look around, he runs over to us and stops gasping for breath. He makes to give his report but I stop him. "Catch your breath, warrior." I instruct him. He nods and after a few deep breath, straightens up. "Captain, I beg to report that there is a large clearing in the trees eight hundred paces to the North West. It is large enough for a camp with a good line of sight. There are three approaches and good thick tree cover." He delivers it quickly and then steps back waiting for orders.

"Excellent warrior, rejoin your unit. Battle Master, an extra ration for this loyal brother. Kē-phās, recall the other scouts and prepare to move out. Yĭ-ăn-nī and Yă-nnī take a squad of warriors and mark out the route. I shall be along with My-rōn and Nīk-ă-tōr can bring up the wagons. To your posts." The group breaks up and while the horns sound to recall the scouts I join Kă-llī-ōpē and My-rōn. Confident in the abilities of Nīk-ă-tōr and with Kă-llī-ōpē on my arm I follow Yĭ-ăn-nī and Yă-nnī. Before long we have reached the clearing. There is enough space for a full war camp and Yĭ-ăn-nī is already marking areas for the tents, while Yă-nnī is flagging. The two trees that have grown in the middle of the clearing, which will need to come down.

"Well it seems we are not needed. There is nothing else to be done until we get the tools and manpower." I remark. Kă-llī-ōpē turns to me and puts her arm around me, "Does this mean you can spend some time with me?" I turn to My-rōn, "Well, how do you like that, she claims she has been neglected. I ask you My-rōn, does she look like the sort of woman who could be ignored?" My-rōn, a man of many with his own woman, smiles and replies, "I am too old to be involved in this."

"So much for your help. You make it sound difficult to be with me." Kă-llī-ōpē smiles innocently. "That is just cheating. Who could resist such an innocent face," I smile. "I tell you My-rōn, I did not realise the trouble I was taking on. Not that I am complaining." We are interrupted by the arrival of the wagons. Before long the tents are being strung up and the warriors are collecting the saws that will be used to fell trees for fire wood. "We shall go to watch those trees being felled. They may have trouble - they are very tall." I say to My-rōn. Kă-llī-ōpē rolls her eyes, "He moans about me being hard work yet trouble attracts him like a moth to light." I smile, "What can I say. I like to be useful in trouble."

As we walk away Kă-llī-ōpē puts her arm round my waist. "I would ask you to promise me never to take any huge risks but I know that would be pointless. I would just ask you to do the best you can." I stop and smile, "I will try hard, my dear." She smiles back and leans in close to me. I stop and embrace her. She hugs me, holding me tightly as if she is worried she might lose me. Her chin on my chest, over my heart, my head resting on hers. A horn and shouting sounds and the moment is shattered, trouble. One of the trees in the middle of the clearing is swaying dangerously. The saw has nearly cut through it and I watch in horror as two of the restraining ropes snap. The horn sounds again and the warriors panic and run away from the tree. A few remaining warriors cling to the remaining rope. I shout for more men to join them. I start running as the tree sways again. "We need more men on the ropes. We have to make sure it does not fall." I reach the rope and loop one around my arm to grip it firmly. More warriors run to man the ropes, but it is too late. "There she goes. Run for it." Somebody shouts. With creaking and cracking the tree reaches its tip point and over it goes. The warriors holding on the rope are not strong enough and most scramble for safety. Some of us refuse to let go and are dragged over the snow. The tree lands heavily, branches breaking. I fall heavily, there is a ringing in my ears. Somebody grabs me and dazed I struggle to sit up. Kă-llī-ōpē is talking to me but I cannot understand her. She sees I cannot understand and shouts at me. "Are you hurt? What were you thinking? And I after I just asked you to think carefully." I give her a dazed smile, "I must have missed that part. Anyway it turned out safe. I am still alive." She gives me a watery smile, "You were lucky. One of the wind warriors was dragged into the tree. His back was snapped." A grunt of pain brings me to the present. "What was that?" I ask. Kă-llī-ōpē looks over to the tree, "A branch has come down on one of the War Gang Masters, it look like he has broken a leg. You were very fortunate." I try to get up. She pushes me back, "No, you sit back and rest." "Pardon me but I have to stand up. It does not do me good to sit on the floor. Makes me feel like a child." I stand up slowly but reel as I reach full height. Kă-llī-ōpē is quick to pull my arm round her shoulder and supports me. "Just take it carefully." She says. "Yes dam." I mumble.

The tree is moved and the other felled. The rest of the camp is built but the atmosphere is dampened. Our new home has claimed its first price of blood. I wonder how many more surprises are awaiting us before we have conquered this land, or will it prove untameable? The ramparts are built, the ditch dug one pace deep and two wide, with the soil piled on the inside. The dead man is buried deep under where the camp will be. After he is buried we settle down for the evening meal. The first fires are lit using wood from the felled giants. I rest on my cloak spread over the ground next to the fire. Kă-llī-ōpē lies next to me, head on my chest, My-rōn is scribbling up his findings from his scouts. Nīk-ă-tōr and Kē-phās are stretched on the floor, enjoying a pre-dinner snooze. "Why was that warrior buried under the camp?" Kă-llī-ōpē asks.

"It is an old tradition in the Ninth. They claim that all their warriors stay on guard and protect their camps even after death. There were rumours in the time of the Elders that when a Ninth camp was overrun by Night Shadows their very dead rose up to fight for them. True or not they fought back and won the battle. Since then all of their dead have had the honour of being buried under their camps. Under their main camp there are vaults for warriors that have died in service." My-rōn comments, glancing up from his work. "Night Shadows?" Kă-llī-ōpē questions. "When our Elders first conquered our land, creatures roamed it killing livestock and preying on our people," I tell the story handed down to me by my Sire. "Our people hunted their lairs down, burned them to the ground and killed them as they fled. My Grandsire was killed by one not long after my Sire was born." There is a moment's pause. Kă-llī-ōpē has rolled over to look at me as I stare into the fire, My-rōn and Kē-phās are watching me intently, only Nīk-ă-tōr remains snoozing, already having heard the story. "The stories are not often told now. Many have forgotten them. My line included." My-rōn comments, "I never managed to talk to your Great Grandsire before his life breath left him. Did he ever mention what the Night Shadows were?" I cast my mind back to his stories and ramblings. "He never described them. It was always too sore for him, having lost his only heir to them. He did however mention a few things. They were large and powerful with long teeth and claws, they were hunters and deadly. They were trouble. He talked in his sleep once. He rambled about an ambush. They were moving to a new lair at night and were attacked. All he said was claws, teeth... death." I feel Kă-llī-ōpē shiver, through the cold or in fear I know not. I resolve not to speak of the horrors at night. "These are not things to be spoken of at night," Kē-phās murmurs "Call it a warrior's superstition." Nīk-ă-tōr wakes with a grunt and grumbles, about being hungry. I roll my eyes to Kă-llī-ōpē who grins. "Story of his life." She whispers, eyes shining and skin glowing in the fire. Nīk-ă-tōr sniffs, "Has anyone else noticed the smell from these pine logs? It smells much better than the fuel we brought with us."

"That's because you leave the logs with your goats." Kē-phās mutters, eyes twinkling in the fire. "Did I hear someone mention something?" Nīk-ă-tōr inquires. "That is what I thought." He curtly remarks when Kē-phās looks elsewhere. "I shall go and see what is keeping the food." With that he gets up and walks into the shadows. "I hope they have enough for him." Kē-phās speaks. "I heard that." Nīk-ă-tōr's voice sounds from the gloom.

The night passes quietly. The sun sets, darkness creeps up and the sentry lighting is lit from the main fire.

Camp life begins early, just before sun up a scout horn sounds the morning wake up, as the sun rises, warriors tumble out of their tents excited over the prospect of a day exploring the trees. There is a general mumble of conversation as the men prepare. I stand before them to issue the day's orders. "War Gang one will accompany My-rōn to map the width of forest. War Gangs two and four will remain here on guard. War Gang three will accompany myself and Yĭ-ăn-nī travelling on the North track into the forest. War Gang five will escort Yă-nnī and Kē-phās taking the eastern path. Those are your orders and you are to return by sun down. Dismissed and good hunting."

I return to my tent to fetch my cape. I find Kă-llī-ōpē putting on her cape. "I assume you will be coming with us?" I ask while attaching the fur to my armour. "Naturally," she replies "where else is a woman's rightful place except by her man's side?" With that we leave the tent to join our warriors standing ready in the fresh morning air. It does not take us long until we are marching the crisp snow. We march until midday and then we reach a clearing in the forest with three other tracks. We stop here for lunch. We have not seen any signs of life. "It seems strange that this place is so silent." Kă-llī-ōpē remarks. "It is too quiet if you ask me." Yĭ-ăn-nī agrees. "Does it concern you?" I ask. "It does, but I cannot think why. It is probably this place. I was brought up on the open slopes so thick forests are always strange for me. I do not like not being able to see a distance." He replies. On we march, taking the middle track deeper into the forest, after setting markers so that we can find our way home. I walk on ahead with Kă-llī-ōpē until we come to a track that has crossed ours. Marks are in the snow, plain for all to read. I call back to Yĭ-ăn-nī, "What do you make of these?" In the snow are large round prints. "I have never seen prints like these before." Yĭ-ăn-nī remarks studying the prints carefully. "The creature was very heavy judging by the depth of the tracks. There was also more than one since there are different size tracks. They were also tall, judging by the tree."

"What tree?" I ask looking around.

"That one." He remarks without even looking up as I look where the tracks lead to and see a branch knocked hanging by a strip of bark. It is twice my height off the ground. "Fair point. What else can you tell?"

"Well I would guess this is a peaceful grazer. The tracks have no claws only blunt toes. They would be better diggers. What really confuses me is how there seems to be something pulled over the tracks. For about a half pace either side of the tracks there are marks. It could be a tail?" He stands giving his report. "I suggest they would be safe to follow." He adds reading my thoughts. I smile, "In that case we shall follow them."

We follow the prints, the track grows narrower and there are more branches broken off, proving something large had pushed through. "Looks like you were right Yĭ-ăn-nī. How did you learn your skills?" I ask while we walk, the ground now steeply sloping up. He pauses for a moment, "My bloodline began as humble goat herders. We grazed in the high mountains above Headquarters. We had some of the best animals, but many wandered. We learnt very quickly how to follow trails. By the time I was born we had learnt much. We also had sold our goats and moved into tracking missing livestock and persons. Wait a moment." He stops looking up ahead then hurries forward. I follow him and come skidding to a stop as he crouches to examine an animal spoor. "What do you see?" He asks. I reply "I see something that will really mess up my shoes." He laughs, "Firstly it is fresh. There is still some heat coming off it. Secondly it is full of spikes from the trees. If this belongs to our footprints we definitely have a plant eater. Finally there is plenty of it, so it came from a large animal." He stands. "Incredible," I remark. "Now that is real skill."

Our thoughts are broken by a sound, from behind us, the creaking of branches. We both freeze and I hold up my hand to stop the warriors. They stop and I motion for them to crouch and fan out. Without a sound they take up their positions. I look left then right, I whisper loudly "Scatter take up cover in the trees. Remain still until I command." The group splits in half and before long are concealed either side of the track. I look around, then duck under the pine branches. These grow lower than ones we have seen before, so we can only wait. For a while there seems to be nothing, then another branch creaks. Yĭ-ăn-nī moves next to me, "Something is coming up the track." He murmurs. "How can you tell?" I whisper. He puts his finger to his lips and crouches to the ground. He puts one hand on the earth and closes his eyes. I follow. "Clear your mind and concentrate." He instructs. At first there is nothing then something, but I cannot tell what, then again and again. Like a pulse. "Footsteps?" I ask. He nods, "Something big." I motion for the men to uncover their spears and raise their shields. I catch the eye of the War Gang Master on the other side of the track and show him the spear head. He nods and turns. Meanwhile the vibrations are clear now, without touching the ground. I move to look out from under the tree, but Yĭ-ăn-nī pulls me back. "Wrap your scarf over your face and keep low. It cannot know you are here. We do not know what it will do." I nod and carefully edge out, squirming along the ground. I look down the track but nothing is there. The track dips down, I glance up the track then look back. A tuft of brown hair appears for a moment before dipping back down under the ridge, the vibrations stops and a branch creaks. What in this world was that? I look to Yĭ-ăn-nī beside me frowning. He shrugs. The vibration starts again. Something is moving. A wonder appears before my eyes. A long face appears large and covered in brown fur. There is no mouth to be seen but the nose is strange, stretched and covering the front of the face. The eyes are small, barely able to be seen under the thick fur. The head rises up further and the creature gets closer. The nose is grows longer. Attached to the sides of the skull are two horns, thicker than a man's hand, which grow sideways before curling down. The tips I cannot see. Under the horns are two small ears like little flags, twitching back and forth. The creature continues to grow taller the head has fully appeared. The creature does not seem in a rush, giving me more time to study it. The shoulders have appeared now, hunched up behind the head. It stops and suddenly flings its head back, to make a sound like a breathy horn. I see the nose is longer than a man, covered in thick coarse fur apart from the very end which has lips. Either side of the nose, the yellowing horns continue to lengthen, pointing first down then pointing forward then the very tip curling up. Now the nose is thrown back, the teeth and mouth are visible. They are level and stained yellow like an old mans. Out of the mouth trails lengths of twigs, the remains of a snack. The creature has stopped, only the head and shoulders in view, turned to one side as if listening. It waits for a moment and then a response is carried on the wind. The same badly blown horn call, and the creature is off again. This time it is walking forward with purpose. More of it rises above the ridge, the height is astounding and then its head vanishes from view, the pine branches obstructing my view. And still it grows. Its coat is dark brown and coarse, arranged in coils like ropes. Finally it reaches its full height the head well out of sight, although the last part of the nose is still visible. The coat reaches the ground in fact the matted strands drag along behind it, creating the swish marks we could not read. I cannot see the legs, and all I can see of the feet is occasionally a front toe poking through the coat. Blunted, yellow toes like Yĭ-ăn-nī predicted. It draws level with us and slows to a halt. It turns slightly towards us, and above us the fir branches swish and sway. I look to Yĭ-ăn-nī who mimes eating and holds his hand out begging me to stay still and quiet. He presses himself close to the ground and I copy. The brown nose appears above my head and I freeze the end of it curls round a branch and pulls it. The gap created shows me the head, the jaws moving slowly and the small ears gently swaying. The eye is clear now, about half the size of my fist and a deep brown colour. It rolls around then slows to a stop until it is looking at me. I will it to keep moving but it stays looking at me. Its nose stops and moves to me. It moves closer and closer, but all I can look at is the deep, strangely sad eye. A tree creaks up the track and the creature pulls back surprised. The pine branches spring back to place and all I can see is the feet again. The creature turns back and suddenly rumbles. Its calling but something more than that. And then without warning the creature takes off, something so big and yet so fast. It gathers speed running up the track the coat swishing back in the wind the front legs clearly visible pumping away. It is not exactly running, more walking very fast. Then it is gone, a fallen branch blocking my view. Without a thought I scramble out onto the track where all I can see is the animal's pumping shoulders, pounding rump and swinging tail whipping from side to side as it swings round the corner. We can hear it crashing on down the track, rumbling now as it fades into the distance. I run a hand through my hair. Letting out a big breath, I look around now that everyone has emerged from hiding. "It seems that we are not alone." I remark. Dazed Yĭ-ăn-nī says, "That is putting it mildly." The War Gang Master whistles, "That thing would make a mess of camp, it would toss us around like dolls."

"Then let us be thankful that it only eats plants and appears peaceful." I reply. The Master nods, "Shall we go after it?"

"We might as well. We have the time." I comment, after a moment's pause. "Once we turn that corner we are heading back towards the edge of the trees. It will be easy to find the camp from there. Let us go, time is wasting. We had better jog if we want to catch up." The Master gives a curt order and we take off, over the snow jogging up to the corner. A tall warrior reaches the corner first and stops, I just skid round the corner and keep running. The tracks are clear for all to see. The stride of the creature is enormous, he is still moving at speed. We keep jogging for a while. Yĭ-ăn-nī, being more used to long runs, takes the lead and suddenly he crouches, sending the warrior behind him skidding to the side. Yĭ-ăn-nī looks up at the tracks, "He is slowing down. The stride is shortening. We are gaining on it."

"Then stand up and keep up." I say as I run past. Kă-llī-ōpē, skipping along next to me, starts laughing, her eyes shining with excitement. "Having fun, dearest?" she gasped. "I would not miss this for anything. I wonder what the others have found." I replied. "How does he keep doing that?" I manage to say as Yĭ-ăn-nī tears past to take the lead once again. As he goes past he shouts over his shoulder, "You are soft, that is what it is. Wait, hold here." We skid to a stop breathing heavily. "Did you hear that?" He asks turning to me. Before I can ask what the sound was, it becomes obvious. Over the wind is the shrill trumpeting higher than before. "It must be just round that last corner." Yĭ-ăn-nī whispers. "Only one way to find out," says Kă-llī-ōpē and begins to walk forward. I stutter and look toward Yĭ-ăn-nī who grins, "So that is how things work."

"I tell you if she was a warrior she would have been flogged by now," I comment. "She will get in trouble one of these days."

"I think she is more than capable of looking after herself. Pity the person who crosses her path." Yĭ-ăn-nī said in wonder. "You can be sure of that." Was all I could say before walking to the corner.

Kă-llī-ōpē reaches the corner, she stands near a tree and looks carefully round. She seems amazed. Just before I reach her the rumbling and trumpeting begins again. Eager to know what is happening I pick up the place. The picture before me is incredible. The track has led us back to the clearing where we stopped at midday. We went straight across and took the north track and we have come back to the passage that went east. In the middle of the clearing is the creature along with seven others. The one from the track with dark brown fur is there, the largest of them. Apart from one fairly small one, about the height of a man, the rest have white coats. Two are nearly the size of the large brown coated one, the other smaller, one sports a snapped horn. The others are noticeable smaller. One is digging, churning the snow into mud. Others are pulling at the trees, keeping their jaws turning. The tallest white coated one is standing in the centre of the clearing swaying gently. The other warriors arrive and I motion for them to crouch. "Yĭ-ăn-nī, is there any way you know of that they can sense us?" I whisper to him. Yĭ-ăn-nī thought for a moment, "The wind is in our faces so they cannot catch our scent, as long as we can keep quiet and fairly still we should remain safe. What are you planning?"

"We have to stay here until they move so that we can take the track home. I do not want to disturb them. I doubt we can go through the woods without making noise or losing our way." I reply. "I just hope they move before sun down." I look up; the sun has long crossed its high point and dropped a good distance, we do not have time to waste. "I reckon we have a quarter of a day of light left. Tell the men to fall back to the path and be ready to move when the way is clear. You, Kă-llī-ōpē and I will wait here watching them. War Master take the men back and keep them quiet." I hissed the orders.

The sun continues its journey across the sky and the creatures show no intention of moving. Then the large one in the middle gives a strange cry, one of fear and pain. The others are quick to respond. They stop what they are doing and move over to it. They encircle around as if shielding the white one, holding out their noses as if trying to talk. The white one in the middle suddenly swings round facing away from us, and bellows again and the brown coated creature we saw on the track starts to do something strange. It stands up on its hind legs, coat blowing in the breeze balancing for just a moment at full height. It must have been six or seven times taller than me. Then it drops from that height, his front legs pounding into the ground. The vibration is incredible. I had been crouching but I was knocked over, the ground bucking underneath me. I sit back up and then it does it again. Down he crashes and up he goes doing it again and again. Suddenly the white one with a single horn joins in swinging itself up and then crashing down. The ground quivers and shakes as if living. Before long all are doing it even the little dark one, so that there is a constant thud from where one is hitting the ground. The white one in the middle suddenly crouches and strains, trumpeting shrilly, a brown bundle of fur, glistening and steaming falls into the snow. The others stop and begin trumpeting. I look at Kă-llī-ōpē in awe, "We have just seen a giant being born." The mother has now turned round and is passing her nose over the brown bundle. In fact all of the creatures are nuzzling it as if greeting the newcomer. One passes in front of it blocking our view. The mother trumpets and the others take a step back. We can see it again. A leg paddles the air as if the baby is finally adjusting to its new life. A squeal sounds from the bundle and the mother rumbles reassuringly. Eventually all the legs are paddling and I cannot help but smile at the poor creature. The mother however knows what to do. She reaches over with her nose and gripping a leg she pulls the baby over until rests on its chest. She rumbles and then the baby answers in a shrill scream. It pulls it legs under itself then straightens its back legs leaving his chin on the ground. It is too comical and I have to smother a laugh as it tumbles back into a pile on the floor. It squeals indignantly about being dropped in a heap. The mother again rumbles encouragingly to it and once more it valiantly rises. This time both front and back legs are very wobbly but holding it up. The poor baby stands shaking. His nose flops around, he seems unable to control it he shuffles one foot forward then the other. He starts to tip over but his mother comes to the rescue using her horns to support the newborn. The baby again shuffles forward, more confident now. One leg slides away, the baby squeals and the mother catches it. Before long the baby is walking rather than shuffling. The brown creature raises his trunk and trumpets. The group move off up the northern track, the mother and baby bringing up the rear. The sun sinks low over the trees and the shadows swallow up the creatures. The way is clear.

I pull the horn from around my neck and give two short blasts. There is a jangling behind us as the warriors turn the corner and move over to the home track. I look longingly back to the northern roads imagining the secrets still to find. It is time to go back to the camp. As it is we shall be late, and have to hurry. I am eager to hear how the other parties did.

The sun sinks much lower and the shadows are much deeper before we can see smoke from our camp fires. As we arrive horns are sounded to signal our approach. We halt and break formation outside the camp. Dinner is in full swing. However there is a surprise. A smell that I am unfamiliar with hits my nose. A very rich and meaty smell hangs over the camp. Nīk-ă-tōr greets us a plate of meat in one hand, a knife grasped firmly in the other. "What kept you, we may have finished all the food without you." He greets us. He wafts the meat under my nose and I cannot help but stop and sniff the delicious meat. I can feel my stomach groan and I realize how hungry I am. My mouth is watering from the smell. "Sit yourselves down by the fire and we shall find some food for you."

He hustles us to the fire and what a sight meets us. Over the flames, roasting gently is a huge joint of meat. It has been started but much still remains. "What is it?" Yĭ-ăn-nī asks. The

Wagon Masters move around us giving out plates of meat. The smell is intoxicating. The meat is firm and greasy and very hot. I blow gently on it trying to make it cool enough to eat. There is the crispy skin which crunches and crackles when eaten. Then there is meat slightly tough but very juicy. I eagerly gobble down the meat, two helpings; three and then four. At last I sit back wiping my mouth and beard on the back of my hand and enjoy the heat of the fire. "Now that feels good." I murmur. Kă-llī-ōpē after having a modest third helping, sits next to me on my cloak. I put my arm round her shoulders and hug her close. "What more could a man ask for?" I murmur sleepily. "You are too easy to please." Kă-llī-ōpē replies kissing my cheek. A shadow falls over us, "Look at this anybody would think they were on leave." Nīk-ă-tōr chuckles. "Space for a little one?" he asks and squats next to us on the cloak.

Kă-llī-ōpē sits forward, "What have you been up to this time?" she pull his hand forward to examine a bandage. Nīk-ă-tōr shrugs her off, "It is only a scratch. I suppose I had better tell you what happened. We left the camp and walked until just after midday. The track opened up and the ground was covered in tracks like the ones we found near the camp before we climbed the Wailing Pass. They had been digging and routing around. We managed to find some that lead away into the forest. I had the warriors spread out and follow the tracks. After tracking them for a while we heard squealing and digging from ahead. Sneaking forward we saw many of these creatures in a small clearing. They all had black bristly coats apart from the smallest which had brown pelts with white lines. They all had white manes of hair down their back which they could raise and lower like spikes. The older animals had long white hairs growing from their snouts. Also the males had teeth that grow around the snout. They were obviously prey animals the way they were nervous of the slightest sounds. I decided to catch one for dinner tonight. I spread the warriors around to encircle them. We decided to go for one of the old large males. I blew the charge and we attacked. Most turned and ran for it but in the confusion we manage to separate a large male. We had to hedge him in with the shields to keep him from savaging us. He was a real fighter. We surrounded him, stabbing where we could and all the time he was kicking, charging us and trying to bite us. He was ferocious and dangerous. He managed to push his snout under the shield of a young warrior and flip him over. He then gored his chest going through the armour like twigs. All the time we were stabbing away but it did not work. That pelt was so thick and after we found he had a layer of fat underneath. In the end we had stab him though the eye. He twitched for a long time after. We only cooked half of him today so we then had this huge animal to walk back to here. It was Kē-phās here that had the idea of how to bring it back to camp." Kē-phās took up the story after cleaning his fingers on a rag, while Nīk-ă-tōr went back for more food. "I managed to cut down a nice straight branch. I had to use a small saw to strip the branches back. I tied the legs of the creature together they slung it on the bar. We used to use it when the ground was too rough to use wagons. Anyway we had to use six men to lift it. It took us all afternoon to walk it back. Anyway how was your day?" We sit up late talking about our discovery. The sun is well set and it is near the second watch when we eventually reach our bed. Warm and holding the woman I love close, it does not take much time to fall asleep.

CHAPTER 8

I AWAKE WITH A start. I do not know why. Beside me Kă-llī-ōpē stirs then settles back to sleep. I settle back down trying not to wake Kă-llī-ōpē up. I close my eyes waiting to sink back into sleep. A shout breaks the silence followed by a scream. Within moments I am up and pulling on my shield and spear. Kă-llī-ōpē is awake and I tell her to stay in the tent as I duck out. The scene before me is strangely calm. The camp is still. I crouch shield forward and spear up. I can see no one, Kē-phās emergences from the next tent with spear and shield. "Did you hear that scream?" he asks. "Yes I did, where are the sentries?" I reply. He looks around, "Now you mention it there is something wrong."

"Check that side of the tent I will take this one. I am going to call out the guards." I move and pull my horn to my lips. I blow a high note and a low note, three times. I hear the noise of warriors rousing themselves. Then Kă-llī-ōpē shouts urgency in her voice, "Behind you." I spin on my heel just as a shadow launches itself at me. I fold my knees and hold my shield up the shadow hits my shield squarely where my face just was. The impact knocks me flat, I spring back up but the shadow has gone into the night. "Alarm, alarm. The camp is under attack. Turn out the guard." I shout. Warriors pour out their tents. "Take up defensive positions in between the tents. Beware the shadows." It does not take long for them to take up their places. Mountain warriors up from shield to shield, wind warriors waiting behind. "I was attacked and the sentries are missing do a head count." I instruct the War Gang Masters. Kă-llī-ōpē arrives with her coat of rings on carrying mine. I take a moment to put the rings on. "Assign two men to ignite the outer fire rings. Let us have some light to see properly." Time passes and nothing happens. Nīk-ă-tōr arrives at my side dressed for war. "I have missed this." He remarks. Kē-phās twitches my arm, "We are missing ten men including the War Gang Master with the broken leg. He insisted on taking a watch. How could they have vanished? What happened?"

"I sent you to look around and something tried to jump me. If Kă-llī-ōpē had not warned me it would have had me. It was aiming for my face. It was fast and strong." A sudden shout draws attention. "Captain, Captain contact." A warrior shouts. The Battle Master shouts back, "What did you see?"

"Movement in the trees and glowing lights." The warrior replies.

The Battle Master shouts, "Pick up your visuals." I walk over to the warrior.

"Where and what did you see?" I ask.

"There was movement and then two white glows just for a moment and then they turned away." He replies not looking away from the forest. It is the young wind warrior. I step back the Battle Master tweaks my sleeve.

"He is young and nervous." I turn to him, "Nervous is good, it keeps you alive."

"Perhaps they have finished for the night?" At that moment a savage roar splits the air.

Shadows spill out of the forest running for the camp, growling and snarling, snapping and howling. "Here they come," shouts the Battle Master "Shields up and do your worst." The shadows stay on all fours, low to the ground, run towards us and rear up at the last minute. Teeth shining in the fire, claws bared. The silence shatters into clanging on metal as the shadows crash into the shields. There are grunts and cries as the warrior struggle to remain on their feet. There are shouts from the War Gang Masters to fight and hold the line. There is a savage shriek as a spear digs home ahead of me. The man quickly withdraws his spear to fight again. A man slides down and is overwhelmed by the shadows. He screams horribly and is dragged out of the camp before he can recover. The gap is sealed by the warriors before anything can get through. A cry rings through the camp, "We are being overrun, they are breaking through." All along the line the walls of shields are being broken up. "Break contact and withdraw to the fire." I shout. The men frantically thrust out their shields then turn and run for the fire. I shout to rally. One warrior, who is not fast enough, is pulled down and torn to shreds. There are glowing eyes everywhere, white teeth glint in the fire. The element of surprise lost, instead now they stay beyond the light of the fire. They circle round, growling, waiting, malevolent. "Come on then," somebody shouts, "are you scared." I take charge, "Right, I have had enough of this! You shall leave our home. You are not invited. Light Muster launch your spears at them." The Battle Master throws his arm high in the air. "Light muster, let fly." He shouts, down go his arms and like a broken veil up go the spears. There are screeches and howls as the spears find their marks. "Again!" I shout, encouraged by the result. Again the spears fly and again the shadows screech and howl. One savage shadow peels off and charges out of the shadows. A mountain warrior lunges and spits it on his spear, kicks it off and recovers. "One last volley and charge." There go the spears and the horn sounds the charge. With a shout and rattling of shield on spear I run forward aiming to hit the shadows surrounding us. Beside me a warrior slips and a shadows jumps on him slashing at his shield. I stab the beast, it screams and falls on its side twitching violently. I have no time to see if the warriors survived, two shadows leap towards me. I aim my spear at one and slam my shield into the other one. My spear must have found its mark for the shadow howls, but my spear is stuck and I cannot free it. All I have to protect myself is the shield. I hunch behind it, desperate to avoid the creature on the other side. A warrior to my side stabs the creature in its throat, killing it. I only have a moment to notice the white trim of Kă-llī-ōpē's cloak before she is off chasing the shadows again. It seems we have hit them hard, for the shadows are fleeing. "Chase them away and re-group at the camp fire." I shout, stabbing wildly at a twitching shadow. Across the camp there is shouting and the noise of battle as the final shadows are run out of the camp.

A howl stops the warriors and the last of the shadows turn tail and vanish into the forest. Everyone hurries back to the warm and light of the fire. We have been hit hard, out of the eighty or so men we started with only half that number still breathe and some of them are not doing well. The first light of dawn reveals the true extent of the night's fighting. The Battle Master presents a bleak report, "Almost all of the wind warriors are dead or dying, mostly from blood loss, only one light war gang master and four warriors will recover. Of the wagon haulers only six have survived, the wagon masters are both missing. They were hit hard; the first attack fell hardest on their side. Also Dry-ăs is dead. I have given his surviving plans to Nīk-ă-tor. Only one of the Mountain War Gang Masters has survived. Twenty two Mountain warriors will survive; two are beyond help and will pass soon. Most carry injuries, one has lost an eye. Two of the tents are useless torn to shreds; it seems they went after the food. I recommend we abandon this camp and make for the Wailing Pass." He finishes and stands straight. He carries a series of cuts across his face where one creature attacked him.

I pace back and forth in the snow, weighing the options and considering what to do next. I walk towards one of the creatures killed in the fighting. Only three bodies were found, once the sun had risen. I crouch next to the largest, studying the creature, trying to understand it. The creature is large; when alive it would have reached my waist and could have easily swiped for my face. It is covered in the thick fur that seems to characterize animals from this area. The main part of the pelt is white with a grey mane running down its back. It has thick shoulders and front legs, heavily covered in muscles. The back legs are strong but shorter, tilting the creature upwards. The feet are wide, the soles covered in fur keeping them warm in snow. The claws are surprisingly small, really only points buried in the thick fur. The tail is short and stubby, with thick fur. What truly sets my teeth on edge is the face. The head is long and large, it has a wide nose below deep set eyes. The brows protrude, casting the forward facing eyes into deeper shadows. The jaw is wide with immense strength and power. The teeth are long and pointed, yellowed with age. The front teeth are chipped, with some gaps. Four teeth in two pairs, protrude far enough for the lips to close behind them. They are long, much longer than my hands width. They are very sharp and pointed, not to be trifled with. This is a creature designed to kill. I stand up and look at the forest, a movement catching my eye. This fight is not over yet. They are still out there. "Yĭ-ăn-nī, what can you tell me of these creatures?" I ask, not taking my eyes off the forest. Yĭ-ăn-nī takes a moment to collect his thoughts before answering, "Judging by the body they are ambush creatures, they are too heavy for long runs. The fur matches snow so it can help to give it some cover. The teeth are incredible and I would hazard a guess that they use them for slashing rather than biting. Most of the injuries on the warriors would support that. They must kill by weakening their prey then waiting. The claws would also help with this." He must see the confusion on our faces for he stoops to one of the bodies and pulls a leg up. He presses on the pad and the claw springs forward, making us start. He continues, "This makes sure they keep sharp and are not worn out with walking," he pauses and sniffs the air. The smell of blood is thick. He then sniffs his cloak. "The smell of the roasting meat must have drawn them in. The smell is also on us. They think of us as food. If we can remain in open ground we will not have much cover but we cannot easily be surprised." I nod and think some more. "We shall abandon camp. We shall take our wounded and retreat to the Wailing Pass. We have achieved our aim. We know this land can be inhabited but we have currently do not have the numbers to do this. We shall return to Headquarters. We must try and cover as much ground as possible before nightfall. Whatever these creatures are, they dislike light. I do not like the idea of being exposed and having to fight them again." As the sun rises we break camp in preparation to leave. The wounded report to the Battle

Master to have their injuries bound. Almost all carry cuts from the night. The Wind Gang Master organizes the few surviving provisions into packs to be carried back with us. Kē-phās joins me after a long cut on his arm is bound up, "A difficult night's work. I watched over Kă-llī-ōpē during the fight, but she did not need it. She fought like a warrior." I nod my thanks, "What of the twins?" Kē-phās smiles, "No need to worry they are both fine, only minor scratches."

"Like that minor scratch of yours?" I ask. Kē-phās looks at the bandage.

"I stabbed at a shadow and another caught me as I pulled my arm back. Do not worry my arm will heal, the creature's head will not." He smirks. I take my leave to join the column of warriors forming ready to leave.

There is a snarl from the forest. Everyone stops and looks towards the sound. Nothing can be seen in the trees. I look round, thinking quickly. "Move move," I shout pushing the warriors nearest me "We are leaving now. We must go." The Battle Master senses the urgency and begins shouting. Before long the column is ready to march and I order it forward. We walk past the camp one final time, most dipping their heads, remembering their fallen comrades. We pick up the pace marching quickly towards the edge of the forest. I walk at the front. Yĭ-ăn-nī beside me keeps looking around. A flash of movement to my left catches my eye, but when I look there all is still. I look back to Yĭ-ăn-nī who nods and leans in close. "I fear they are trying to flank us. They may try to stop us leaving the forest depending on how brave they are feeling. We must make sure we stay as one big group. They will kill anyone who becomes separated." I raise my voice so that all can hear, "Keep formation at all costs. If you are separated, you will not survive. Battle Master, pick up the pace." The clanking increases as we march faster. There are more shapes in the forest both on the left and right. Ahead the track straightens out letting us see the edge of the forest. Upon reaching it, I cautiously raise my hand and halt the column. Open ground. I shiver nervously at the thought of being caught out in the open with these killers. From behind there is growling. The warriors look around. The more injured look nervous understandably, for if they cannot keep up they will die. I look back to see movement in the trees either side of the track, the growling becomes louder as more voices are added to it. "Time to move again," I shout over the growling. "Do not look back, run for the rocky outcrop. Keep together." With that final command I put my head down, running for the rocks a short distance from the trees. The jangling of armour increase behind me as the other warriors run for safety.

Breathing heavily I reach the rocks and scramble up them. Behind me the others reach safety and I lean down pulling warriors up into the rocks. Kă-llī-ōpē slightly flushed from the running gives me a smile as I pull her up. Only when the warriors are all safe do I look back to the forest. It stands silent and intimidating. There is no sound or sign of the night shadow. I turn my back on the forest, breathing a sigh of relief. Beside me Yĭ-ăn-nī keeps watching the forest. I raise my voice, "It seems we are safe for the moment."

Yĭ-ăn-nī pulls at my arm, "You spoke too soon." He whispers. I look back to the forest with a sense of foreboding.

At first all is as before, I look back to Yĭ-ăn-nī for answers. Then shapes begin to slink out of the forest, walking into the sunlight. Close to the ground, watching us and ready to kill. They snarl and snap at each other but still they creep closer. Over twenty shapes have emerged from the forest and more are still coming. "Yĭ-ăn-nī," I ask "what can we do?"

He turns to me a note of concern in his voice, "Nothing we can do, we must flee." I turn back to the warriors, "Retreat to the Wailing Pass." I blow my horn and jump for the snow. I wait for all the warriors to start running. A large shadow creature climbs onto the rock outcrop. It is larger than the others and instead of charging me it looks down on me. The others take up places on the rock. The rest of the warriors are gone running over the snow, with a final look towards the creature I turn and run after them. I look back but instead of chasing the creatures wait on the rocks. The largest creature, their leader, throws its head back and lets a roar loose that chills the blood in my blood. The rest of the creatures join in then charge down the rocks after us. I shout a warning to the other warriors. I catch up to the main group, shouting for them to keep together. The Night Shadows catch up with us in no time. They split up; some run left and others run right funnelling us together, stopping us from changing direction. Others continue to run behind us forcing us to keep running.

A gruelling race begins. On and on we run forcing our aching muscles to keep going. Well aware of what will happen should we stop, we would be overrun and slaughtered, our one hope is to reach the pass and retreat to safety. For two leagues we continue this Death Race. A warrior stumbles and only just manages to keep his feet. Another carrying a heavy injury collapses in the snow, exhausted. I grit my teeth and keep running. Before long he is over-whelmed and disappears under claws and teeth. The exhausted warriors forget their pain and run on. A further two warriors have fallen before we can see the pass. The creatures seem to sense a change for they begin baying. They run closer almost snapping at our heels. Some run faster and skid to a halt in front of us trying to stop us making for the pass. Their leader takes centre, crouching ready to lead the charge against us. I roar my defiance for the creatures, raise my shield and run for the large night shadow. The warriors around me forget their fear realising that they have to break the creatures to take the pass. With a roar the creatures charge us.

Man and beast crash as with shouts and howls we collide. The leader runs straight for me. I hold my shield forward and run at him howling in rage. He launches himself at me, mouth open baring his fangs and teeth. At the last moment, I pull my head down as the world explodes in light, the creature hitting my shield and the rim hitting my helmet making my ears ring. Desperate to see clearly again, I shake my head. My sight returns as the creature circles in front of me, tail sweeping left to right and a growl in his throat. I stand my ground looking in his eyes. He stops and crouches only paces away from me. The battle around me I am oblivious to, I am focused. The creature stalks forward slowly putting his feet down, the long claws creating deep marks in the snow. Then without warning it springs, roaring ferociously. I instinctively duck presenting a smaller target. He continues to fly at me claws out, teeth gleaming. I raise my heavy spear and the creature twists to the side avoiding the point. Its dreadful teeth nearly ripping my arm, its shoulder covered in wiry fur pushes past me spinning me round and knocking me over onto my back. It lands lightly, skids round in the snow and crouches ready to attack once again, then stalks forward. My spear knocked out of my hand lies beyond my reach, the best I can do is pull my shield closer waiting for it charge again. Maybe this is it.

But it is not to be. Behind me a warrior shouts and launches himself at the creature trying to distract it, his black cape swirling behind him. The creature turns to face him. The warrior crouches and stabs forward. The creature twists past the spear before jumping at the warrior. In a flash the warrior disappears under claws and teeth. I have to act.

I struggle to my feet and grab my spear. The largest creature is roaring, baring its red stained fangs. Warriors attack the leader, who now finds itself out numbered, roars and leaps at a wind warrior, pushing him down. Instead of killing the fallen warrior it bounds away over the snow roaring all the time. I look around me for the first time since fighting the leader. The ten remaining Night Shadows are fleeing, running away. Some warriors jeer and shout at them. Others are simply exhausted and slump in the snow. Three warriors are lying in the snow not moving. Yĭ-ăn-nī is crouching in the snow leaning over a body, his back to me. I walk closer, the fallen warrior wears the black cape of the Royal Guards. I can see clearly now Yĭ-ăn-nī's back is heaving. I reach him and sigh deeply. I place my hand over my heart and then put a hand on his shoulder. The fallen warrior is dying, blood wells from his torn chest and mouth. He struggles to speak his lips twitching and then he stops still, his life breath failing. I look back to Yĭ-ăn-nī watching his eyes fill and his mouth move in silent words. The dead warrior at his knees is Yă-nnī.

The cries of victory soon die as the battle fire wears off and tiredness once again overcomes us. There are at least eight dead, one creature still breathes, its chest rattling and quivering. Kē-phās raises his spear above it and then stabs down into its chest, silent and sombre. It struggles briefly, rising up before its final breath escapes and its eyes glaze over. The other creatures have fled; I instruct two warriors to watch for their return, the mist is thin. The rest of the men dig in the deep snow. They dig through the hard earth using their spears. The dead are buried and stones placed over their graves, so that they are not disturbed. The final thing to do is mark the grave of the fallen Royal Guard. I stand over his resting place gripping his spear in my hands I thrust it into the sky, then with a grunt drive it between the stones. The spear point glints in the sun. I kneel before the grave, place my spear in front of me and then place my fists on the ground. I hold the warrior's bow honouring a fallen warrior. I then stand and step back. Yĭ-ăn-nī steps up and kneels to his twin. He stands up and walks away, his face empty.

I look up at the sun, warmed by its gentle caress. I feel a hand take mine. Kă-llī-ōpē stands next to me her head on my shoulder, she looks tired. Neither of us speak, we just enjoy the sun and being close. "Yă-nnī did a brave thing, he saved me but died doing it. That is the path of a true warrior." I remark. "I thank him with all my heart. I find it fascinating that only having known you a while he is willing to sacrifice his life for yours." Kă-llī-ōpē remarks not moving her head from my shoulder. Nīk-ă-tōr walks up behind us, his shield arm bandaged. He seems content to watch us, I look at him and he nods to the Pass.

"We should move before night begins to set." He remarks.

"We shall start in a moment. Form the remaining men up, make sure they have plenty of layers for the journey home." I reply. Kă-llī-ōpē looks up at me and I smile at her. She smiles wearily at me.

"I shall be glad when we return home." She murmurs.

"If we still have a home left." I reply.

"You think we may not?" she asks frowning.

"I do not know. But I know this; if we are to survive we shall have to return to this place. I just hope the other scouting parties met with success. I do not like the idea of taming this land." I remark.

A horn interrupts our thoughts. The warriors are starting to form up ready to descend the Pass. "I suppose we should join them." I say. Kă-llī-ōpē moves her head and we both start walking to the column. The Pass as ever is wreathed in mist. As we walk into the mist the sun fades, visibility is reduced. The warriors become nervous, the battle still fresh in their memory. The Walls of the Pass emerge from the gloom. I breathe a deep sigh and Kă-llī-ōpē next to me squeezes my hand. I throw back my shoulders and proudly walk towards the Pass.

Descending the Pass is easier than climbing it. The wind now behind us pushes us down. It is almost as if it is happy to speed us on our way. The snow is still thick but instead of slowing us down it makes us almost slide down the Pass. Beside me Kă-llī-ōpē slips and I quickly grab her. She smiles at me, putting an arm round my waist. I pull my cape round making sure that it also shields her from the cold. She huddles under it smiling gratefully for the extra warmth. The wind continues to blow and we struggle on fighting for balance and control on the loose snow. More than once I have to steady myself against the rocky Pass. We reach the middle of the Pass where the rock walls separate out to form a large cavern. The warriors are exhausted by this point and near collapse. I call a halt and the men gratefully fall out and lie out on the snow. Many wrap themselves in their cloaks and close their eyes. The Battle Master cries to them, "Do you want to freeze? Group together. If you do not you will die." The men obediently shuffle closer together. I collapse on the snow letting Kă-llī-ōpē bury herself in my thick furs. Once she is comfortable I turn on my side throwing my furs over her to keep her warm.

She smiles at me, "I always thought you were an honourable man." I look back to her.

"I am only obeying the Battle Master." I remark laughing. She rolls her eyes and kisses me on the cheek.

She rummages in a fold of her cloak, "I made this for you. Something for you to remember me by." She pulls a pendant from a pocket. I take the twine in my hand. Hanging from it is a small carved woman. It is no longer than my hand and is beautifully carved in dark wood. The hair of the woman is silver locks of Kă-llī-ōpē's fine hair. The face is delicately carved with eyes, nose and mouth. It is a real work of beauty. I marvel at it lost for a moment at such an exquisite gift. I proudly slip the twine over my head, the carved woman hanging over my heart, next to my stone token from the Supreme Ruler.

"Nīk-ă-tōr was kind enough to carve it for me. He says the likeness is quite accurate." She says.

I think for a moment then reply, "I must disagree with him. Your beauty could never be captured by something so simple as wood." Kă-llī-ōpē blushes a deep red, her beauty shining clear as the sun at midday.

"It is lovely." I murmur and kiss her gently before laying back.

"Wear it as a charm to keep you safe." I hear her say.

"With you beside me I need nothing else." I reply.

I am awoken by somebody shaking me. I open my eyes to see Kē-phās leaning over me smiling. I nod to him and he moves away to wake the rest of the warriors. I gently wake Kă-llī-ōpē up then sit up and yawn feeling stiff, but surprisingly warm after lying on the snow. Most of the warriors are still resting. I notice Yĭ-ăn-nī sitting apart from the group. I have not heard him speak since he found his twin. I stand up leaving Kă-llī-ōpē my cloak, shivering slightly as the wind bites through my armour. I crouch beside him in the snow.

"How is it with you?" I ask gently.

"How does one cope with the passing of a twin? We were closest to each other." He replies sadly.

"And to die so far from our land, there will be no one to watch over him, or to remember him."

"Your twin will not be forgotten, he sacrificed his life. If no one else will remember him I will. I and my heirs will sing long of the man who gave his life to save mine. His honour will last for many life times. I do not think you need to worry about him being undefended. I have a feeling we shall return before long. In meantime I need you here with us. You will achieve much and be a fine warrior with much honour. Never forget him, do not be afraid to live without him." I council him. After listening to me he lifts his head nodding slowly, agreeing with me. He smiles with silver lines down his cheeks and I pat him on the shoulder before going to see the Battle Master who is talking to Nīk-ă-tōr.

"We are making good progress. Is the map safe, Nīk-ă-tōr?" Nīk-ă-tōr moves his cloak to reveal a tightly bundled roll of skin hung from a rope around his neck.

"In that case let us descend with all possible speed." I remark, leaving the two to continue their conversation. I walk by the lines of warriors that are rubbing their muscles to life.

The wind is still blowing as we start walking down the next passage. We walk for a long time, the sleep has helped us to recover some of our energy, but we are still tired. Before long the same feeling of weariness begins to seep back into our bones and muscles. Our steps, once confident and energetic, soon fade into trudges that barely lift our feet off the ground. We turn the corners in the Pass always hoping that it will be the last turn and more often than not seeing another passage. My eyes are heavy and once or twice they fall shut. I shake my head trying to keep awake. I pull a handful of ice from the passage, trying to use the cold to wake myself up. It does not work and my eyelids once again fall shut.

Next thing I am aware of is a dull ache on the back of my head and someone shaking me. I sit up confused at finding myself on the floor.

"What happened?" I mumble.

"You fell over and slid down the Pass. The only reason you stopped was the corner." Kē-phās says leaning over me. I struggle to my feet. I look his shoulder and my heart jumps in my chest. I shakily point over Kē-phās' shoulder.

"The Pass, we have reached the end." I groan. Kē-phās turns to look over his shoulder and then calls for the other warriors. Eagerly they flood down the Passage, excitedly skidding round the corner to gaze at the end of the passage.

Before long we are on the way home. The mood of the warriors changes, they become happy, almost playful. They tease each other but all are pleased about the prospect of being home; of being safe. The mist swirls round but gradually thins out the further we march away from the Wailing Pass. I clasp Kă-llī-ōpē's hand, my head feeling better all the time. The wind is picking up, blowing towards us, swirling the mists round as it collides with the wind being funnelled down the Wailing Pass. We march about three leagues, the mist becoming more of a blizzard. Winter has come to our homeland. Over the howling of the wind a fell tune is carried to us. Out of the snow shapes began to form, shapes that wail and walk like the dead. All the warriors raise their shields and weapons expecting an attack. Instead the mist lifts to reveal a long column of men and women. At their head dressed in black walk twelve men. Upon their shoulders they carry a man and woman, led by a Battle Master. In front of them walks a single man playing a Double Long Horn. It is Hy-pă-tōs, he is not playing happily, rather his notes quiver and fail. He seems unable to play properly and now I see why. I fall to my knees weeping, unable to stand as I realise who is being borne aloft on lamenting shoulders. I could not believe that they could be gone. Ruler Krē-ōn and Sovereign Ă-mǐn-tă are dead and this is the lamenting cry:

> *Woe to us for eternity,*
> *Weep at our loss and lament.*
>
> For we have lost our Wise Rulers,
> We have lost our heart and soul.
> Our Elders forsook us,
> And left us with no hope.

Woe to us for eternity,
Weep at our loss and lament.

Our warriors are spent,
The blood of our men spilt.
Our women scattered,
Their beauty fled away.

Woe to us for eternity,
Weep at our loss and lament.

Our children are screaming,
They are scared and unprotected.
They weep for their dams and sires,
But they cannot be comforted

Woe to us for eternity,
Weep at our loss and lament.

The winds are moaning,
The mountains tremble,
The skies are red as blood,
Lit by the fires of death and war.

Woe to us for eternity,
For our foes are returned and victorious.

"Is it possible? What has happened while we have been away?" I ask Hy-pă-tōs.

"How are you still alive? It has been so long. We assumed you had been killed like the rest." He replies.

"How did this all happen?" I ask, almost afraid of the answer. The rest of the column has halted now. The other Royal Guards have come up to the front to see what has happened. They look relieved to see me. The Battle Master signals the column to halt and fall out. The warriors look haggard, tired but above all distraught. Most sit staring at the Rulers or at our group. I am worried. There are only eighteen men including myself that now carry the black capes of the Royal Guards. I stand, "What happened to the Rulers?" I begin. The Guards look at each other until Tō-bĭt stands.

"Not long after you left, the Supreme Ruler and Sovereign announced the arrival of an heir to the Royal Bloodline. The Sovereign began to show signs. Everything seemed to be going fine until late one night. The Sovereign was taken ill with a fever and died." Tō-bĭt stops here wiping a tear from his eye. "I am sorry but I have watched over the Sovereign for many years. I was one of her protectors as she grew up. I cannot believe she is dead." He slumps back down on the ground.

"The Supreme Ruler was devastated," Rhă-mă takes up the tale. "He retired to his throne room and mourned for many days. Also at this time there were many reports of attacks and unrest. Bands of marauding enemy soldiers roamed the land, we never had any descriptions or accurate numbers. We lost contact with the scouting groups and we have not heard of them since. We assume they are all dead. There is no way down the mountains. The reports were delivered to the Supreme Ruler, but nothing was done. He was deep in his grief, refusing all comfort not even eating. Meanwhile the attacks became worse. No survivors, they never attacked the villages or headquarters but they devastated the surrounding land. Not long later the Supreme Ruler was found dead in the throne room. There were no signs of violence. The Elder council took charge in the absence of an heir. A confirmed report was presented to the Elders of a large body of enemy soldiers making for Headquarters. The Elders called for an evacuation. We abandoned the settlements and made for Headquarters. It was the only safe place. We only just made it in time. Two nights after we left the skies were red with flame and the moon covered by smoke. They burned the settlements. They cannot be far behind us, if they followed us quickly. We are planning to make our final stand here..." His voice trails off.

I stand up, "We are devastated by the news, I must bring my news directly to the Elder Council." This news settles heavy over my heart as we march back to Headquarters. The pace is fast but the warriors are silent and gloomy. We reach

Headquarters quickly and I call the few Royal Guards together that have not gone to entomb the Rulers. "Gather all the able bodied men and make sure they are armed." With that I leave the group and head for the Elders Council. I am challenged by the sentinels on the main door. They level their weapons at me, until I pull the white stone with my name and rank from under my armour. They instantly level their weapons and stand to attention. The War Gang Master, standing at the flap, raps on the iron knocker and ducks through to inform the Council of my arrival. It takes a long time for him to reappear. In fact, I am starting to wonder what is happening when he finally returns from the tent.

He stands to attention, "The Council have voted to deny you access to the Council Chamber." I stand for a moment trying to comprehend the response. I focus my eyes and must be frowning, for he nervously flinches under my gaze. I again pull out my stone name tag.

"You will take this in and display it for the Council to see." I order. He takes the token and goes into the Chamber one again. This time he comes back quicker looking uncomfortable.

"The Council have voted to deny you access to the Council Chamber." He insists. He hands back my name token, I pull on my Empty Face and prepare for battle. I do not like the way this is going. I check left and right. Kă-llī-ōpē is behind me; Kē-phās stands to my left; Nīk-ă-tōr stand next to Kă-llī-ōpē and Hy-pă-tōs is standing to my right.

"Follow me, we are going to war." I order. Without hesitation I order the War Gang Master to stand aside. He takes one look at me, the other beside me, then looks at my face and stands aside. As I go past he murmurs, "May the Elders protect them." I smile harshly at that, then my face re-arranges itself.

The inside of the Chamber is dark compared to the reflected light off the snow. The talking dies down as I enter. It is dead by the time they have recognized me. The atmosphere can be cut with a knife as the other Guards arrive. There are eight counsellors, two from each bloodline. The two councillors from the Ă-kay-dăs look happy to see me, both having known my Sire. The others councillors look less than thrilled, two look angry. One of them now stands.

"By whose authority do you force yourself on this Council?" He asks, barely keeping his disdain out of his voice. I look at him, one of the Kōr-ăx Councillors, an old stubborn warrior past his prime. I take a moment to consider my answer, letting the pressure build, making the Councillor fidget in his chair. I hold the token up for all the Councillors see.

"I believe you recognize the seal of Supreme Ruler Krē-ōn. I was given this by the Ruler. I believe it gives me some standing amongst our people."

The Councillor raises a hand and interrupts me, "You have a piece of stone given to you by a dead Ruler. The Sovereign is also dead. There is no heir, the line of Rulers is broken. You are released from your oath. You currently hold a basic military rank and only a minor civilian class. You are therefore intruding on this session; you have no rights amongst these proceedings. You shall leave this tent or you shall be removed by the Guard." The councillor finishes his speech and sits down, unable to keep the pleasure of victory from his voice or eyes. I look at each of the Councillors in turn; the two Ă-kay-dăs representatives now look angry at the flagrant disregard for honour and tradition. Most of the others avoid my eye. One maintains eye contact then looks away quickly. Only the old Councillor from the Kōr-ăx looks me firmly in the eye.

I can feel the fury from the other guards and out of the corner of my eye see Nīk-ă-tōr step forward to deliver his own scathing remarks. Much as I would love for Nīk-ă-tōr to put the old Councillor, in his place I motion for him to stop and then step forward. "I am fully aware of the rules of the Council; my bloodline was present at the first meet. We have been servants of the Rulers and the Council since the beginning. If I remember correctly, my blood never spoke of your bloodline. That maybe because your bloodline has only just attained the rank of Councillor. When we were first serving the Council, you were tending goats in the High Plains. Do not teach me my place amongst our people; I am fully aware of my rank with the passing of the Ruler." I pause at this point, judging the effect of my words on the Councillors. The Kōr-ăx Councillor is looking uneasy at my new attack. The Ă-kay-dăs look confident, the other Councillors are look unsure, the old Councillor may have bullied them into his mindset. I begin again, this time on a different argument, "Why are the warriors preparing for battle? There is no reason to stay here."

A Councillor from the Heir-ăx interrupts me, "How can you say there is no reason to stay? Where shall we go? Up into the mountains to freeze on the deep snows? Our crops will not grow and our flocks will die. And where have you been? You have been missing for many days. Why should we listen to your advice?" the Councillors mumble their assent. I wait for them to quieten down before I reply.

"I do propose that we go up into the mountains. I have just been up there." I take a moment to enjoy the surprised look on the Councillors. "Some days ago, I requested that the Supreme Ruler, the former Ruler Krē-ōn dispatch a scouting party to the mountains. He agreed and dispatched a convoy under my command to map the high mountains. We managed to climb the Wailing Pass and found thick forests with pine trees larger than any I have seen before. There is plenty of flat land, excellent for building. The crops can freeze and the flocks can die for all I care. There are animals aplenty to hunt." I stop again letting this new information sink in. The Councillors look unsure, I push ahead while I hold the initiative. "We are being chased out of our homeland but we can have a new homeland. We must leave for the High Mountains. They are much richer than these lands, with the extra resources we can fight off any invasion."

The Kōr-ăx Councillor speaks up much less confident than before, "And what of dangers? With all those animals there must be some predators. Will we any better off there than here?" The Councillors look back to me, waiting for me to answer. I swallow the hardest part of my argument to arrive. "When we conquered these lands we had to defeat the Night Shadows. Indeed my bloodlines were responsible for destroying most of them. They must have escaped to the higher mountains. We were attacked and hunted; they claimed over half of my warriors. Eventually we had to retreat."

I stop here, the Kōr-ăx Councillor looking around in final triumph. "You lost half your men, trained warriors. Was that just through the Night Shadows or through inexperience? It does not sound like our chances of survival are better than staying here." I look at him, angry at his suggestion of my incompetence. My patience finally snaps and I turn on the Councillor, my eyes burning, "Have you lost your courage? Or maybe you are just soft in your old age. How can you have audacity to sit there and question either my judgement or ability to lead? Instead I was elected head of the Royal Guard; that must say something for my skills. If the Ruler was here you would not presume to question my judgement. You cower like an old man." He squirms back from my wrath. The other Councillors look on, not helping the Kōr-ăx Councillor.

I step back and start pacing in front of the Council. "What is better to stay here and face certain annihilation either from starvation or being slaughtered? Or to move to the new lands where, I cannot lie, we shall be hit hard but at least we shall have more chance of survival. If we go in a large group the Night Shadows may hesitate to attack us. However a decision must be made, I await the Councils judgement." I stand still, hoping I have done enough.

One of the Ă-kay-dăs nods and stands, "Thank you for making our options clear. Leave us now while the Council decides our next action. We shall inform you of the outcome shortly." I bow and take my leave, instructing the others to follow me.

We do not go far, I pace outside the tent. The waiting is painful, the time seems to pass so slowly. Eventually, Nīk-ă-tōr puts a hand on my shoulder to rouse me. I blink, surfacing from my deep thoughts. "You did you best, I am sure the Council will make the right decision. That Kōr-ăx Councillor just likes to throw his weight around, he is all cold and no bite. The two Councillors from the Ă-kay-dăs are good honourable men. They will fight your argument." I nod and sit down, only realising how tired I am when my muscles ache and eyes close.

Nīk-ă-tōr wakes me up, "The Council are calling for you." I stand and stretch before pushing the tent aside and entering the Council. The Councillors are looking flustered and tense. There must have been some heated arguments. The Kōr-ăx Councillor is looking angry, arms crossed sitting back in his seat. I hope this is a good omen.

One of the Ă-kay-dăs Councillor stands, "The Council has decided, after much discussion to abandon the homelands and make for the Wailing Pass." I breathe a sigh before he continues, "Furthermore the Council has decided to put you Āi-ās, in charge of the rear guard. You are to collect all the trained warriors who have male heirs to continue their bloodlines. You will also have all the former Royal Guards at your command." He then sits. I bow low to the Council, "I obey" I reply simply. I bow and leave.

The camp swarms with activity. There are many rumours of the new homelands and fears over the journey. I send the Royal Guards calling for warriors. Before they leave I give them a message, "Guards, I only want volunteers, force no one to join us. Make sure anyone who joins us has an heir to continue his line. Yĭ-ăn-nī stay with me, I have a special task for you." I let the others move off to collect support, "Yĭ-ăn-nī I must ask you to have no part in the battle, you must stay with the Council. They will need you in the Mountains with your skills."

He bows low, "I obey commander. Thank you, it was an honour to serve under you."

"I am sure we shall see each other again." I reply mystified by his answer.

He shakes his head, his face pained, "If the enemy are following, they are going to fight hard to catch us. You will be hard pressed to keep them back. Then there is the issue of them simply following us up the Wailing Pass. How do you intend to stop them?" he asks.

I step back and walk back and forth, "I was thinking of that. The rocks on either side of the Passage looked unstable.

If we could collapse them, they would block off the Pass. The mountains either side are impassable. Even if that did not stop them, it would give us enough time to make our escape."

Yĭ-ăn-nī looks at me a sadness in his eyes. "It is a good plan but there are many risks. I do not envy you." A horn sounds across the camp. The column is ready to move once again.

This time the atmosphere is lighter, the people more hopeful of survival. I stand to the side with my three hundred warriors or so. My people take what they can carry and stream out of the gates towards the North. We are waiting for the end of the column to form the rear guard. While we are waiting, the two Councillors from the Ă-kay-dăs join us.

I thank them for supporting my argument, "That is fine. You had the right argument and that Councillor needed reminding of his place. We knew your Sire; think of it as repaying an old debt to him." With that they join the column.

Before long the end approaches and I order my new command to join the column. I take a final look behind me at the silent fort. Then with a sigh I turn back to the marching. We make good progress, but it will take us two days to reach the Pass. As darkness falls on the first night we stop unable to make any progress. I walk through the column which simply stops being too large to form a camp. The atmosphere is good, moral is stable. People are talking about the new lands. The air is rife with rumours. There is also nervousness and excitement. I sit and sleep with Kă-llī-ōpē until I am shaken awake by one of the Guards.

"Captain, you must see this!" with that he leads me to the rear of the column. The dark sky is a glow behind us with orange colour. Many of the men are staring in wonder at the colours.

One asks, "What is it?"

"Fire," I reply bluntly, "Our homes are being looted and razed to the ground. They will chase after us soon." The air around me falls silent as many look towards the sky now watching the smoke that billows over the sky.

The next morning horns sound across the camp waking us up ready to move off. I take my place next to the column again waiting for the end to arrive after the steady trickle of stragglers from the previous day's march walk past my command. A runner bounds across the snow making for our position.

He bows low to me, breathing hard, "There is a large snow blizzard coming our way, from the south." I look back past the end of the column which is now in sight.

"That is not a blizzard," Rhă-mă standing next to me comments, "The pattern is all wrong. Normally the wind blows a wall of it forward." Indeed this blizzard looks like it is rising from one spot.

"Of course, it is not a storm but battle formations." I realize the truth and turn back to the runner, "Run back to the Council and tell them we are being followed. Tell them to make for the Pass with all speed. It is imperative they make all speed to reach there quickly." I turn to Rhă-mă next to me, "Sound the alarm, make this column move faster and set the rear guard."

Before long the column has picked up its pace. They flee towards the Pass, dropping anything that may slow them down. The civilians panic and most break into a run. They are understandably nervous. There are not enough warriors to protect them all. They keep glancing behind them making sure we are still protecting them. I look behind me, the snow trail is coming closer, gaining on us. There is a commotion ahead and I halt the rear-guard to prevent them from crowding the column. I also send a Royal Guard with two warriors ahead to find out the problem. They return before long. "The head of the column has reached the Pass. With so many people crowding the narrow passage it will take time to let everyone pass. I run a hand through my hair, trying to figure out what to do next.

"Rhă-mă, take ten warriors and form a contact web behind us; I want to know when they come close." He nods and calls for a section of wind warriors to follow him. He leads them back the way we came.

Time passes, the enemy comes closer, and the refugees begin to panic. They crowd forward, crushing and pressing trying to reach safety. The snow being kicked up is nearly on top of us by the time we reach the Pass. The last of the refugees are making their way into the path. I order some of the warriors to attach ropes to the loose rocks around the Passage ready to collapse the Pass. The Passage is narrow at this point; there is only space for fifty warriors side by side. I arrange the warriors in six ranks the first two Mountain warriors and the back four ranks wind warriors carrying many spare spears. I stand at the rear supervising the rock falls. Though the formation I spread the Royal Guards to keep moral high. I make sure Kă-llī-ōpē is standing up the passage where she will be safe. She is not happy but at least she yields and stays put. Not far up the passage I see members of the Council, including the disgruntled Kōr-ăx Councillor. He looks at me and sneers. I turn away disgusted. Instead I turn to the preparations for collapsing the Pass. The ropes are in place and I confirm with the Battle Master in charge his orders.

"Unless we are over run you are not to collapse the Pass until we are safe. Understand?" He nods "And on not account are you to let Kă-llī-ōpē come past." I add before pulling on my helmet. A horn sounds and I push my way through the ranks. The warriors under Rhă-mă's command are returning, running over the snow to cross the open ground. They take their places in the formation. Rhă-mă is not with them.

"He stayed to continue observations," a warrior sent from him informs me, "none of us saw what was coming. The snow being kicked up is too thick." The entrance to the Pass is a raised levelled mound. We cannot see the ground past where the earth sinks. The snow trail is crawling ever closer. Soon we shall be able to see the enemy. I sound prepare on the horn. The warriors stop their talking and re-align their ranks, spears are readied and shields fastened. Helmet visors are lowered and armour is tightened. We are ready, come what may.

The thick snow, huge and menacing, has arrived. The men are moving restless around me. A strange horn sounds, like nothing I have heard before. It is a sharp note, it makes my spine tingle. Then we see Rhă-mă and the other warriors, running for their lives, heads down not looking back. Now we see why; from below the ridge runs a band of Night Shadows. Howling for blood they chase after Rhă-mă and the other warriors. From up and down the ranks there are cries of encouragement. They have a long run over three hundred paces. An older warrior lags behind as the younger one sprints out ahead. The creatures are gaining quickly on the slowest runner, who sensing his fate stops and turns, raising his spear to meet the creatures with iron and shield. He does not last long cut down by two of the creatures with tooth and claw. Baying for more blood, the creatures run faster now, the smell of blood driving them on. There is a collective groan as Rhă-mă stumbles and is overrun by the nearest creatures. There is only one left now.

Ty-phōn next to me groans, "He is not going to make it." Indeed the creatures are closing in on him, his face full of terror. Then a horn sounds and the creatures break off. They turn back and gallop back down the ground until they have dropped out of view. The young warrior continues to run, glancing behind him he slows to a jog and then exhausted stumbles and falls in the snow. I run forward with warrior next to me, grab his shoulder and run back to the ranks. I push through the front ones calling for space. The warriors move aside, letting me reach the rear rank. The wind warrior, not much older than a child, is slung over my shoulder exhausted. I gently lay him on the snow. He breathes slower now, he mumbles between gasps. I lean over him to try to understand him.

"Must run, not safe." He mumbles.

"Easy, easy, you are safe here. What did you see?"

He sits up, "I saw hundreds of them, a whole army. Then those creatures saw us and gave chase. The main force will be with us soon." A horn sounds and there is a shout from the front.

I move to stand up but the warrior grabs my arm, "Wait there is worse, those chasing us were the small ones. I saw men riding larger creatures. I could not see them they were too far away and their faces were covered in veils." There is more shouting from the front.

"Rest, then find your way up the Pass. You have earned it." I instruct the young warrior before pushing my way back to the front.

"Let us see what they have to throw at us." I remark to Ty-phōn. "Careful what you ask for." He replies, not taking his eyes off the ridge.

A horn sounds again and suddenly there is movement. Over the ridge pour Night Shadows. Fifty bound over the ridge and still they come, their white and grey pelts thrashing around as they run. Before long the ridge seems full of them. Another horn sounds and they stop running at us. Instead they mill around the ridge as if waiting for more orders. The movement makes it impossible to count their numbers but there must be hundreds. A fight breaks out amongst them and a whine sounds as one is torn to shreds under the teeth of another. The warriors around me fidget nervously. A horn sounds again and more Night Shadows appear over the ridge. These are different, much larger. They march with more discipline that the other creatures. Perched high on their backs are riders. These creatures are wearing harnesses, they have been tamed enough to ride. Their riders sit tall, carrying long handled reapers, the blades gleaming in the sun. In the other hand they carry a cudgel, presumably to keep a control over their mounts, which snarl and snap, straining at their leashes. They wear long flowing robes, black and covered with mud stains. They show little armour apart from an elaborate plate of metal attached at the neck and hanging over the chest. Their faces are covered by veils hanging from elaborate headpieces. They sit silent and still in their saddles. From behind the ridge the horn sounds again. The top of a standard appears and grows. The warriors around me are silent and afraid. The standard shows a picture of the sun burning and a blackened moon ruling the sky. The group protecting the standard are different from the rest. They do not fear being seen, they were no capes or veils. They are painted with strange patterns and they command a fear from the others. The riders seem intimidated by them, crouching away from them, avoiding their eyes. And no wonder for they look terrifying. They have very pale grey skins. It is hard to see clearly for they are a fair distance away but it looks as though their skin is made up of small squares. Whatever it is, they are not human. All of a sudden they begin to scream and shriek. On and on they scream, each sound making my ears twitch. Behind me I can hear the rattle and clank of armour as someone nervously shuffles around. The fear around me is thick enough to cut. I read the mood of the men and I realise how nervous they are. A warrior takes a small step back. I have to do something before their morale is destroyed, if everyone is taking steps backwards what hope does the formation have of being solid?

I step forward, leaving the ranks before turning to face them, raising my hands, calling for silence. "Be easy, men. We did not initiate this combat, but by the Elders we shall defend what is rightfully ours. Before us stand the tyrants who have snapped at our heels for so long, the disturbers of our peace. We stand here to face them, giving our people time to escape. I do not lie to you the odds are not favourable but I tell you this; by being here, you are carving your place in stone on the history of our nation. We shall be remembered as long as our people survive. So I say let them come, let them come and die. For every one of us that falls they shall pay for it with ten of them. Their victory shall be costly. None of you have my permission to fall before you have claimed ten of their warriors...even then I will not permit you to fall. Show them the meaning of fear. Fight like nobles and be remembered as heroes. Cry Honour for the Elders, Ruler and Revenge." I drum my shield with my spear and around me the warriors take up my cry. We drown the noise of their shrieking out, drumming spears on our shields. I can feel the morale around me building. We are ready.

I send a runner back to see what progress has been made. One of their warriors peels away from the others and walk forward. He is taller and larger than the others, he carries a horn and lash instead of a reaper. He raises the horn and blows a long note, then kicks his heels on his beast making it jump into the massed ranks of the Night Shadows. He lashes at them and shouts at them in no language I can understand, more yelling than words. He points towards us and again wields his lash. The creatures throw their heads back and then start loping towards us. The warriors mounted on beasts stay put but yell and scream in encouragement. The creatures flood towards us, teeth bared and baying horribly.

I shout for the ranks to form up, "Shield Wall, Shields." The front rank kneels, shields go forward, spear tips up and warriors brace for impact. I shout loud, letting my voice carry across the formation, "I have dealt with these creatures before, do not fear them. Light Muster...Prepare to let fly." Behind me I hear the rattle of spears as the Wind Warriors raise their shields. The creatures run closer. A hundred paces, ninety paces, eighty paces, seventy paces.

"Light Muster...On my command." Sixty paces, fifty paces, forty paces, I can see their teeth and hear their claws on the snow. Thirty paces, twenty paces.

"Let fly." Behind me the grunts signal the release of the spears. The shadows pass overhead as the spears fly overhead. The air is full of hissing as the spears dip. The creatures skid to a halt as the sun glints off the metal. Then the shrieks and whines as the spear pierces hide and flesh.

"Again." I shout and another volley flies. The front line of creatures vanishes under the hail of spears, the creatures behind crashing into the ones in front.

"Sound the charge." I yell and without waiting run forward crashing into the confusion, stabbing, hacking, fear replaced by battle calm. All along the line warriors break ranks and pile into the fighting, dispatching the creatures pinned by the spears and push forward. Within moments we have gained the upper hand, and the remaining creatures have turned tail and fled. A wind warrior raises a spear to launch after a fleeing creature but I stop him. "Save your spears, reform ranks, head count."

The first results are good, minor scratches and few major injuries, no dead. The warriors cheer and rattle their shield over the first victory. The man on the large beast forces it into the fleeing creatures, laying into them left and right with his lash. He tries to stop them but they continue to flee. In the end he raises his horn and blows three blasts. Warriors flick their feet and their beasts run into the mass of fur. With neat swipes of their reapers they finish off the routing beasts. Their pursuit takes them over the ridge and out of our sight. We can still hear the squealing and whining. Our warriors fall silent at this show of brutality. Before long the squealing falls silent and the pursuit warriors re-take their places in the formation.

A runner pushes his way through the silent ranks of warriors to my side. "A message from the Battle Master in command of blocking the Pass, Captain. All the civilians are through and are a safe distance up the Pass. At their rate of travel they will not make the new lands for over a week. You may start your withdraw when you are ready." With that he pushes back through the ranks to reach the safety of the pass. I order Ty-phōn to send the two rear ranks of Wind Warriors up the pass, then turn back to watch the silent waiting ranks of enemy. A second warrior carrying a whip instead of a reaper joins the first and they appear to be arguing. I cannot hear the words and I have no desire to. Movement behind me seems to attract their attention. I look behind to see the rear ranks of Wind Warriors turning and marching for the Pass. My muster only number two hundred. I see the problem. In sending warriors away I have weakened my defence, a necessary sacrifice. Now the civilians are clear it does not take long, for the wind warriors to march past the choke point. I turn back to await the enemies next move, toying whether or not to send another rank of warriors after them while there seems to be no movement from the enemy.

Suddenly the ground beneath us shakes. I look back in alarm to see the passage behind us blocked, the snow settling over a massive pile of rocks. Alarm spreads through the muster and I order the Royal Guards to re-establish control, while I establish what happened. I run to the rock fall, livid with rage.

I shout over the rock fall, "What happened?" No reply. "What happened?" I shout louder this time. This time a cry replies, I recognize Kă-llī-ōpē's voice. She is calling my name and I answer her. The only words I can make out are betrayed and Kōr-ăx. I angrily punch the rock at the treachery. A bellow brings my attention back to the battle. I hurry back to the front line. With a roar and horn blast, all of the warriors kick their mounts and swing their reapers, before letting them rest on their shoulders. Instead of a well ordered start the ranks ripple forward without any cohesion.

"Light Muster…Prepare to let fly. Heavy Muster…shield wall. All Warriors brace for impact. They are going to try to over-run us. Hold ranks." I shout, calling the warriors to order. The warriors prepare and fall silent. The mounted warriors continue to walk forward, saving their energy for one final charge. One breaks rank and charges forward. A horn calls and he regains control, the other warriors jeer and call as he re-joins the ranks. When they reach one hundred paces the horn sounds loud and long. The ranks respond and the warriors kick back their heels, reapers held high and ready for blood. All I can see is a line of warriors about to over-run us.

"Light Muster… Wait for every spear to count." The enemy pounds ever closer, the warriors either side of me start to edge.

"Hold steady." I bellow desperately trying to retain control.

"Light Muster…Let them have it." The front rank of charging mounts howls as the spears make contact.

"Again." I shout adding more spears to the chaos.

"Too late." Somebody shouts as the leading mounts, covered in spears trips but continues to slide towards us.

"Brace, hold tight." I shout, seeing the danger of our ranks being broken by the corpses of the mounts flying at us. It is no use. The corpses smash into our ordered lines, the enemy quickly pour into the gaps breaking our formation into many smaller fights.

Two warriors face me, one on the ground, another still a top his beast. I present my shield to one and thrust my spear at the creature's throat. My shield rings as the other warrior smashes into my shield with his reaper. All along the front line we are being pushed back. Our spears are not long enough to reach them. The beast in front of me rears, throwing its rider, I shout and turn to the other warrior. He raises his reaper high, aiming for my helmet. I raise my shield and block the hit. He pulls his reaper back. Meanwhile the other warrior has freed himself of his harness and joins the fight. He raises his reaper high to hit down and again I raise my shield to block it. The blade smashes down numbing my arm from the impact. He tries to pull it back but it has embedded in my shield. There is sound like laughter from the other one as he lowers his blade and swings it back aiming for my side. I quickly stab him in the stomach he leaves exposed. The blade rips through the layer, there is no armour and I stab harder, driving the spear deeper into his stomach. I laugh expecting him to fall back dying, instead there is something like laughter from him. The other starts as well and says something to the first who swings his reaper back. Amazed he is still alive, I pull my spear back but it is caught in the folds of cloth. He continues to laugh and starts to swing his reaper I use my spear to push him off balance. There is a burning in my stomach as the edge of the blade cuts between my armour. The other tugs his reaper and rips my shield from my arm. The other warrior, falling back, has freed my spear and quickly grabs it with the other hand. My shield arm is still numb from the impact. The second warrior staggers to his feet, black blood dripping from his wound. The first warrior kicks the shield from his reaper and raises his weapon. They both swing their weapons. I step forward to avoid one and take the other on my spear. They both reel back and the injured one falls over. I turn my attention to the standing one. He begins swinging his reaper around his head and I step back. Suddenly I lose my footing, tripping over something I land heavily on one knee and look up at the warrior standing over me. He laughs and with a grunt swings his reaper round. The full impact lands on my helmet. The world explodes in light and then all goes black.

I feel cold, something cold lands on my face. The pain comes flooding back my neck is sore, my stomach tingles. I groan and open my eyes. My vision is dark and hazy. Slowly the world comes into focus. It is night time but the moon shines full giving me some light. I sit up bruised and in pain. All around is the stench of death, the smell of blood is in the air. I roll over and vomit, the smells and sights proving too strong for me. Before me is carnage worse than the chaos of my bloodline's slaughter. Everywhere there is blood and bodies. The snow is red and churned up. The very walls of the Pass are stained red. I grip my spear lying at my side and use it to push myself onto my knees. Around me is death and destruction; all the warriors dead and gone. I eventually find the strength to stand, the pain from my head is fading but my stomach still hurts. I walk the field lost and dazed. Every step is pain for me. Every face is a lost warrior. I collapse to my knees beside Nīk-ă-tōr and Kē-phās who have died side by side. I cannot believe they are both dead. I am alone. My people are safe behind the rocks, but I am alone. I walk to the rocks blocking the Pass. I desperately pull at them trying to force my way through to my people and the woman I love, but I cannot, the rocks are sealed. I hit them again and again, all hope fading. I collapse in the snow, tears rolling freely down my cheeks, broken and distraught. I throw my head back screaming my rage to the Elders, imploring them to help but the sky remains black and silent. Pulling my stone token from my neck, I look at it just a piece of stone now with no meaning or purpose. I place my other hand over it and crush it to dust beneath my fingers, letting the pieces run through onto the snow beneath. Instead I take the charm given to me by Kă-llī-ōpē, I kiss it gently and tuck it under my armour. I turn my back on the Pass and my people. My world is lost, burned to ash. I care not for my people, unable to help them anymore, caring not for their honour as they destroyed mine. May those responsible for this betrayal be visited by grief ten times mine, may they be accursed for all time. But for me the curse is worse. The curse of life.

www.ingramcontent.com/pod-product-compliance
Lightning Source LLC
Chambersburg PA
CBHW021730190726
48288CB00009B/2990